M Christmas

by

Kathi Daley

I want to thank the very talented Jessica Fischer for the cover art.

I so appreciate Bruce Curran, who is always ready and willing to answer my cyber questions, and Peggy Hyndman for helping sleuth out those pesky typos.

And, of course, thanks to the readers and bloggers in my life, who make doing what I do possible.

Thank you to Randy Ladenheim-Gil for the editing.

Special thanks to Joyce Aiken, Janel Flynn, Marie Rice, Pam Curran, Kim Davis, Connie Correll, Joanne Kocourek, and Vivian Shane for submitting recipes.

And finally I want to thank my sister Christy for always lending an ear and my husband Ken for allowing me time to write by taking care of everything else.

Books by Kathi Daley

Come for the murder, stay
for the romance.

Zoe Donovan Cozy Mystery:

Halloween Hijinks
The Trouble With Turkeys
Christmas Crazy
Cupid's Curse
Big Bunny Bump-off
Beach Blanket Barbie
Maui Madness
Derby Divas
Haunted Hamlet
Turkeys, Tuxes, and Tabbies
Christmas Cozy
Alaskan Alliance
Matrimony Meltdown
Soul Surrender
Heavenly Honeymoon
Hopscotch Homicide
Ghostly Graveyard
Santa Sleuth
Shamrock Shenanigans
Kitten Kaboodle
Costume Catastrophe
Candy Cane Caper
Holiday Hangover – *January 2017*

Zimmerman Academy The New Normal

Ashton Falls Cozy Cookbook

Tj Jensen Paradise Lake Mysteries by Henery Press

Pumpkins in Paradise
Snowmen in Paradise
Bikinis in Paradise
Christmas in Paradise
Puppies in Paradise
Halloween in Paradise
Treasure in Paradise – *April 2017*

Whales and Tails Cozy Mystery:

Romeow and Juliet
The Mad Catter
Grimm's Furry Tail
Much Ado About Felines
Legend of Tabby Hollow
Cat of Christmas Past
A Tale of Two Tabbies
The Great Catsby
Count Catula
The Cat of Christmas Present

Seacliff High Mystery:

The Secret
The Curse
The Relic
The Conspiracy
The Grudge

Sand and Sea Hawaiian Mystery:

Murder at Dolphin Bay
Murder at Sunrise Beach
Murder at the Witching Hour
Murder at Christmas

Road to Christmas Romance:

Road to Christmas Past

Chapter 1

Saturday, December 17

Santa was dead. There was no doubt about it. His red and white hat was lying at his side, his beard was covered in dirt, and the blood from the large gash on his head was pooled around him. I bent down to feel for a pulse just to be certain, but I wasn't expecting to find anything.

"Did you find him?" Kekoa Pope, my cousin and fellow employee at the Dolphin Bay Resort, asked over the handheld radio resort staff used to communicate with one another.

"I found him."

I heard Kekoa let out a sigh of relief. "Good. Tell Sam to get his red furry backside over to the party. The line to take a photo with Santa is getting longer and longer."

I looked down at the body of a man I knew and respected. My brain hadn't quite reconciled the pounding in my chest with the reality of the scene before me. The whole thing seemed so surreal. "I'm afraid you're going to have to find a substitute Santa for the event," I choked out.

"Substitute? But Sam *is* the substitute." I could hear the panic in Kekoa's voice. The poor thing had been persuaded to take on the organization of the Step into Christmas party even though she had absolutely no background in event planning and was in so deep over her head she'd most likely never see the light of day again.

"I know Sam is the substitute, but I'm afraid Sam is dead."

"Dead?"

"Hit on the back of the head." I looked down at the red bikini I wore with only a grass skirt over the bottom half. I hadn't had anywhere to put a phone, so I hadn't brought mine when I'd gone to look for Santa. "I don't have my phone and don't want to leave Sam alone. Call Jason," I added, referring to my cop brother. "Tell him to bring a team. I'll be waiting near the loading dock behind the hotel."

For those of you who don't know me, my name is Kailani Pope, although pretty much everyone calls me Lani. I'm a WSO—water safety officer—at the Dolphin Bay Resort on the island of Oahu, Hawaii. Normally I spend my shifts on the beach, but this year, just as the holiday visitors began to arrive, half the employees at the resort had come down with the flu, so everyone who wasn't sick had been asked to take on extra shifts. Today I'd spent eight hours on tower two, making sure the guests who preferred to hang out at the surfing beach were both safe and happy, before grabbing a quick shower and dressing in a red velvet bikini, a grass skirt, and an elf hat, to help out as a Santa's helper for the annual kickoff event for the holiday season. One of the main attractions during this time of the year is photos with Santa. When the Santa who was supposed to work the event had called in sick, I'd enlisted the help of my friend Sam, who conveniently owned a Santa suit, to fill in. The sun had long since set, so the alley where I stood was dark except for the overhead lights that had clicked on automatically. If Santa had fallen victim to his attacker in one of the areas that wasn't illuminated, he might not have been discovered until morning.

I watched as the first of the HPD squad cars rolled into the alley. I was expecting to see Jason, but instead it was Colin Reynolds, one of the HPD officers who worked with him.

"Nice outfit. Very festive." Colin winked as he greeted me.

I just glared at the man I'd known most of my life. Colin was a good guy, but he liked to tease, and after five days of sixteen-hour shifts I wasn't in the mood for needless banter, no matter how harmless. "Where's Jason?"

"Finishing up on another call. He sent me to get started. What do we have?"

"Sam Riverton. We recruited him at the last minute to act as a temporary Santa when the man who'd been assigned the job got sick. He's a local I've known for a year or so. He's sixty-six years old, retired from teaching, and a really nice guy. He hangs out with the Monday afternoon senior bingo group I attend with my neighbor Elva."

Colin knelt down to take a closer look at the body. "When did you first notice he was missing?"

"He arrived on the resort grounds at around five. He was supposed to start at six. We arranged for him to get into his costume in the locker room down near the beach that's used by the staff. When six o'clock arrived and there was still no Santa, Kekoa sent me to find him. I started off looking in the locker room, so it must have been an additional fifteen minutes before I found him."

"Is there a reason he might be back here at this time of day? The place is deserted."

"The loading dock staff leave at four and the area is secured. Kekoa thought it would be best if Sam accessed the building by the back door so he wouldn't have to walk through the busy part of the resort on his way to the party. She figured if he could slip in though the back unnoticed he could make a big entrance, so she arranged for the door to be left open."

"How many people knew of this plan?"

I shrugged. "I don't know. Sam's guests, security, and maybe a handful of people who were working the party."

I turned to watch as several vehicles from the Honolulu Police Department pulled into the alley and parked behind Colin's car. I knew most of the men and women who served the community I lived in and it usually gave me a feeling of comfort when they arrived on the scene. Today I just felt empty.

Colin stood up and faced me. "Did you see anyone else around when you got here?"

"No. I imagine whoever did this was long gone by the time I decided to check back here."

"Did you touch anything?"

"No. I felt for a pulse, but that was it."

Colin glanced at the three men who were walking toward us. "I'm going to talk to the medical examiner. While I'm doing that I want you to go back inside and tell whoever is in charge of security to secure the door that leads back here. I'm sure Jason will want to talk to you when he gets here."

"I'll be in ballroom two. I'm helping out with the Step into Christmas event. I'll be there until after midnight, so he can look for me there."

With that, I headed to the back door of the building. It was locked, which meant someone had locked it between the time Kekoa opened it for Sam and now. I turned around and headed back around the building to the main entrance.

I felt like I was in a daze as I walked through the colorfully decorated resort. While Dolphin Bay tends to exude a happy energy on a regular basis, there's something especially magical about the festive sparkle that's created when hundreds of guests gather together in anticipation of Christmas on the island.

Kekoa hurried over to meet me as I arrived at the foyer to the ballroom. "What happened? Who would kill Sam?"

"I don't know." I looked toward the table set for eight Sam had been given in exchange for taking on the Santa gig. My next-door neighbor, Elva Talbot, was one of the seniors waiting for Sam to make his grand entrance. She was going to be devastated when she found out what had happened. "I found him in the alley near the loading dock. Someone hit him in the back of the head." I looked at the hundreds of elegantly dressed guests waiting for the party to begin. "Have you seen Titan?" I asked, referring to Titan Mathews, the head of security.

"Not since this morning. It seems we had another burglary; this time a very expensive necklace was stolen. The last time I saw him, he was attempting to assure the extremely irate woman it belonged to that everything that could be done to find her family heirloom was happening."

"That's five robberies in two weeks."

"I know. I'm afraid we have a real problem."

"I agree, but right now I need to find someone to secure the exterior door leading out to the loading dock. Colin wants to make sure resort staff and guests can't wander onto the crime scene. I'm going to grab my phone and then head upstairs to the security office, but I'll come back right away and we'll figure out what to do next when I do."

"Okay, but hurry. The natives are getting restless."

There was a line twenty people deep at the elevators. The ballroom where the Step into Christmas party was being held was on the second floor of the main lodging and convention building and the main security office was on the fourth, so it was a lot quicker to run up the stairs than wait for the elevator. My long black hair flew behind me as I ran as fast as I could in the red flip-flops that had been part of my costume.

When I arrived on the fourth floor I headed directly to the security office. The only person inside was a new hire whose name I couldn't remember. "Where's Titan?"

"He left for the day."

"When did he go?"

"I guess about a half hour to forty-five minutes ago. I didn't look at the clock. I was on the phone when he came in, did something on his computer, and then left again, but I did hear him mentioning something about having a date he was already late for."

I frowned. "What computer?"

"The one in his office."

I headed in that direction.

"Wait. You can't go in there."

I stopped and turned around. "It's okay. I work here. My name is Lani Pope."

"I know who you are. You're a WSO, and the last time I checked, WSOs don't have clearance to poke around in the security office."

"I guess you heard a man died."

The young man looked shocked. "Tonight?"

"Within the last sixty minutes. I'm supposed to find someone to secure the exit leading onto the loading dock. HPD doesn't want employees or guests wandering out there while they're investigating the crime scene."

"Of course. Just give me a minute."

I waited while he accessed one of the radios we used to communicate among themselves and dispatched the security guard on duty to the loading dock exit. Once that was accomplished he turned his attention back to me. "The door has been secured."

"Great." I turned on my biggest smile. "What's your name again?"

"Bill."

"So, Bill, now that the door is secure we just need to get a look at the security tapes for the last hour."

"I'm not sure I should show those to you. I mean, it's not like you're a cop."

The poor guy looked more than just a little harried, but I needed answers and I needed them immediately. "Look, my brother is the lead detective on this case. He got held up and wanted me to pitch in until he arrived. We're concerned that if we don't identify the person who killed Santa right away he or she will have time to get away, possibly even get off the island. I mean really, what harm could possibly come from us looking at the video feed together?"

"I should check with Titan."

"Do you have a way to get hold of him?"

"I have his cell number for emergencies. Hang on; I'll call him."

I waited, but I could tell by the look of frustration on Bill's face that he wasn't picking up. Bill left a message, but who knew how long it would be before Titan returned his call if he really was on a date?

"Look, time is of the essence here. What possible harm could come from taking a peek at the video feed?"

He frowned. "Oh, all right. What sort of time frame are we looking at?"

"I'm going to say between five-twenty and six. Santa was shown to the locker room down by the beach at a little after five and he was supposed to get to the party by six."

Bill did as I'd asked. I could see his frown deepen as he typed commands into his keyboard. "This is the camera that covers the loading dock beginning at five-twenty."

I looked at the screen he was pointing to. It was focused on the dock and rear door of the alley. Based on the position of the camera and the location of Sam's body, the camera wouldn't have caught the murder anyway. "How many cameras look out onto the alley behind the loading dock?"

"Just this one."

"Can we speed up the feed so it won't actually take a half hour to see it?"

"Yeah, we can do that."

I watched but didn't see much of anything. With the camera positioned as it was I doubted there would be much to see.

"Wait. Stop there." I leaned forward. "Now rewind just a bit."

He did as I asked.

"Stop." I pointed at the screen. "Look here; the door is beginning to open from the inside. Show me the next frame."

Bill tried to do what I needed, but the next frame showed the door closed again.

"Maybe whoever was going to come out changed their mind and closed the door before opening it all the way," he suggested.

"Or not. Go back to the frame where the door starts to open."

He did.

"Look at the time stamp."

"It says five twenty-eight."

"Now go to the next frame."

"Five-thirty."

"So what happened to five twenty-nine?"

Bill frowned. "It's gone."

I glanced at the closed office door where Titan kept a desk. "Who would have access to erase or tamper with the video?"

"No one. The video isn't actually on a tape. It's on the hard drive, which is backed up to the cloud at the end of the day. If you want to review footage of a period of time, you query the video feed by camera number, date, and time. The security personnel on shift can view the feed, but the only people who can edit the video on the hard drive are those with the highest clearance."

"Would Titan be able to delete or alter the material?"

He looked shocked. "I'm not sure."

"Okay, do you remember seeing anything? You've been sitting here monitoring the video cameras. You must have noticed someone coming out to the alley through that door."

Bill looked down at his hands. "My girlfriend called. There may have been a short time when I was distracted."

"How short?" I demanded.

"I guess about twenty minutes. Although it may not have mattered. The video feed rotates. If whatever occurred took place within the confines of a single minute I might not have seen whatever it might have been even if I'd been paying attention."

I just glared at him. "We need to find out if there's any other missing footage. You start looking; I'm going to text my brother."

I noticed several SOS texts from Kekoa when I picked up my phone to text Jason about the missing footage.

"I need to get back to the ballroom. Do you have a cell phone?"

"I have my personal phone."

I jotted down my cell number. "Text me after you've finish looking at the footage. If you see anything, no matter how small, or if you find additional missing footage, text me right away and I'll come back. My brother Jason is with the HPD and I'm sure he'll want to speak to you when he gets here, so don't go anywhere."

I headed back toward the ballroom. It seemed strange to me that the hotel was full of colorfully dressed people chatting and sharing drinks as Christmas carols played in the background, while just beyond the exterior walls a man had been hit over the head and left to die. I couldn't imagine who would want to kill kind, sweet Sam, but I intended to find out.

"I'm glad you're back," Kekoa said when she saw me. "Things are really getting tense. We made an announcement to the guests that due to unforeseen circumstances Santa wouldn't be attending the party after all. Santa's helpers are circulating with complimentary champagne until dinner is served and it seems most of the guests are fine with the situation, but Elva and the seniors are of course concerned about Sam. I'm not sure how much longer I can hold them at bay. They want answers and I think they're about at the end of their patience waiting for someone to fill them in."

I looked toward the table where the seniors were sitting. "I'll talk to them. But not here. Let me see if I can find an empty conference room where we can talk in private. I'll come back to get them as soon as I know where we're going."

"Okay, but hurry. I'm afraid they're going to ambush me if I don't start giving them some answers."

Chapter 2

I located an empty room, then returned to the ballroom to tell the seniors I wanted to meet with them in private. I led them to the room, which wasn't scheduled for use until the following day.

"There are only six of you." I directed my attention to Elva, Janice Furlong, Beth Wasserman, Tammy Rhea and Emmy Jean Thornton, and Greg Collins. "Sam had a table for eight. Who's missing?"

"Susan," Elva answered. "She was here, but her daughter called shortly after she arrived. There must have been some sort of an emergency because she never came back to the table after leaving to take the call."

"I hope her daughter is okay."

"If you ask me, she's a hypochondriac. This isn't the first time Susan has had to suddenly leave an event after receiving a call from her daughter," Janice pointed out.

"She does seem to have more than her share of emergencies," Beth agreed.

It did seem Susan was running to her daughter's aid more often than would seem necessary. Her daughter was an adult after all.

"I think the girl just wants to be the center of attention," Janice voiced.

"Especially since Susan and her husband divorced," Emmy Jean added. "I'd say Susan is trying to compensate for the disruption to the family, so she coddles the girl, which, in the end, isn't going to turn out well."

"Enough about Susan. What happened to Sam?" Elva asked.

I asked everyone to take a seat before I explained as delicately as I could what had happened to Sam.

"Murdered?" Elva cried. "Who would kill Sam?"

"I don't know," I answered. "But HPD is here and Jason is on his way and we're going to figure this out."

"We should do something," Janice, the oldest and most outspoken of the group, insisted. "Sam was our friend. How can we help?"

"When Jason gets here I'm sure he'll have questions for all of you. Answer as completely and honestly as you can. Until then, all we can do is wait."

The seniors Elva socialized with were a feisty group and I knew that in the long run they weren't going to be happy sitting on the sidelines waiting for HPD to find Sam's killer, but for the moment they all seemed to be experiencing varying degrees of shock and were content to wait until someone came to fill them in. Luckily, they didn't have long to wait.

Jason pulled me aside as soon as he arrived. "It appears Sam Riverton was approached from behind. Chances are he didn't even know his attacker was there. We found no evidence of defensive wounds or a struggle. You said Sam was here to play Santa for the Step into Christmas party?"

"Yeah. When the employee who was supposed to play Santa came down with the same flu everyone else has, Sam agreed to fill in." I felt a catch in my throat. "If he hadn't he might still be alive."

"Don't worry. We'll figure out who did this."

"The seniors who came to the party as Sam's guests want to speak to you. They're looking for answers, of course."

"Okay. I'll talk to them before I head back out to the crime scene." Jason glanced in their direction. "Can I use this room for as long as needed?"

"Yes," I answered, "that should be fine. I'll let security know what you're doing.

Which reminds me: What do you think about the missing video feed?"

Jason frowned. "I don't know yet. It bothers me that it's missing. I have a tech guy coming up from the south shore to look at the system. Has anyone managed to track down the head of security?"

"No. Not yet. The guy in the surveillance room said he's on a date, so he might have turned off his phone."

"We'll proceed without him, then. If you do hear from him text me and I'll arrange to speak to him."

"I'm going to call Luke to have him arrange for Sam's guests to have rides home. I know several of them came to the resort with Sam, and even those who drove themselves seem rattled. He should be here by the time you finish interviewing them."

Luke Austin was my boyfriend, who I'd barely seen in the past four weeks. First he'd been in Texas visiting his family and then, by the time he got back, I was busy with all the extra shifts I'd been assigned at the resort. Luke and I hadn't had much chance to catch up, but I knew he'd be willing to do whatever he could to help.

"That's probably a good idea. I may need you to track down some employees for me, so keep your phone close."

"I will." I smiled weakly, then left the room. What I really wanted to do was head home and curl up in my bed, but what I knew I had to do was return to the party and help Kekoa. The poor thing had been running on adrenaline for days.

"What did Jason say?" Kekoa asked when I returned to the ballroom where the party was in full swing.

I filled her in. "I'm really sorry. I know you're shorthanded and it's going to get even worse when Jason begins interviewing the staff, but I need to call Luke to see if he can help me make sure all the seniors who came with Sam get home safely. After that I want to go back upstairs to security to see if the new guy found anything on the video feed."

"It's okay; we'll manage. Making sure everyone gets home safely and finding out who did this to Sam are the most important things right now."

Once again there was a line for the elevator and once again I ran up the stairs. Bill was staring at the monitor with a frown on his face when I arrived.

"Did you find anything?" I asked.

"Yes and no. I can't tell you who accessed the alley through the back door, but I found missing video at both five twenty-nine and five fifty-three. Each time there's a minute missing."

"So someone must have gone out to the alley at five twenty-nine and then reentered the building at five fifty-three. It would have only taken a minute to hit Sam over the head, so I'm going to assume if the person who went out to the alley was the killer he waited for Sam to arrive."

"That's a good theory, but there are other reasons for a person to need to go out to the alley. I know there are some staff members who use the alley for smoking breaks."

It was against resort policy to smoke while on shift. "Yes," I said, "but someone who simply went out for a smoke wouldn't want or be able to alter the video feed. Did Titan ever call you back?"

"No, I'm afraid not."

I stared at the eight monitors in front of us. They each showed a different place in the resort and rotated so that the picture changed every ten seconds or so.

"How many cameras are there in all?"

"Quite a few. I don't know for sure, but I'm going to say at least fifty. There are two or more on each floor and at least one in each conference room and ballroom. There are a couple more in the lobby and several in the garage. There are even cameras on the beach and other outdoor common areas and in the restaurants."

"The places on the monitors rotate between the cameras. Can you manually freeze one of them so that the feed from that camera is shown uninterrupted?"

"Sure. We can manipulate the output from the cameras to the screens in any way we might need."

"Is there a camera inside the dock area? Maybe near the stairs or elevator?"

"You're thinking the person who accessed the back door might have had to pass other cameras along the way?"

"Exactly."

"Give me a minute and I'll pull up the cameras that might have recorded the mystery person."

I waited while Bill typed in commands that brought up specific camera feeds. "I'm going to set the time for five twenty-five. We can take a look at the feed for the next few minutes."

For someone who wasn't sure he wanted to help me in the beginning, Bill was being very helpful now that he'd made the decision to do it. I knew myself how easy it was to get caught up in the chase when a crime had been committed and you found yourself in a race against time to help solve it.

"There." I pointed at the screen.

Bill froze the video feed.

"Back up two seconds and then continue forward in slow motion."

He did as I'd asked.

"Freeze it."

"It looks like a shadow," Bill said.

"Whoever went out to the dock knew how to avoid the cameras, but they must not have taken in to account the shadow they would cast when they entered the dimly lit area."

"There's really no way to tell who it is," Bill pointed out.

"True, but I'm betting the guys at the crime lab can use the shadow to determine things like height and weight. It's a start. Not a great start but something." I continued to look at the video feed from all the cameras as they played across the various screens. "How is it we've had five burglaries in the past couple of weeks without the person responsible being found? It seems with all these cameras it would be easy to see someone sneaking around."

Bill looked away from the screens before answering. "At first Titan didn't believe the thefts were real."

"Not real? I don't get it."

"He said that in his career he'd come across instances when people claiming to have had valuable items stolen from their rooms was lying."

"Why would someone lie about having something like a piece of jewelry stolen?"

"To collect the insurance money or to try to get something out of the resort. It wasn't until the third piece came up missing that Titan began to consider we actually had a problem."

"And then?" I asked. "There've been five robberies that I know of."

"I'm not sure. Titan has been reviewing the tapes, but so far he hasn't found anything. Part of the problem is that the rooms don't have cameras, only the hallways and other common areas. Most of the time the owner of the stolen item doesn't know exactly when it was taken. Like the lady today, with the necklace. She'd put it in the safe in her room five days ago. When she went to take it out today it was gone. It could have disappeared at any point in that five-day period. A lot of people have access to the stairs, elevator, and hallways for the tenth floor."

"I see the problem. Are there cameras that would show who entered and exited a specific room?"

"Unfortunately not for that room. It's a suite, so the door is through a short hallway around the corner from the main corridor. While we did look at who'd been in the corridor there were too many people to come to any conclusions."

I glanced at the clock. "I gotta go. If you find anything relevant to the murder text me. I'd really like to catch whoever did this right away."

It was several hours before I was released to go home. Between serious sleep deprivation brought on by a week of double shifts and the stress of Sam's death, I was exhausted. What I really needed to do was go to bed, but shortly after I arrived at the beachfront condo I shared with Kekoa and my best friend, Cam Carrington, Luke had arrived with Elva.

"Did everyone get home okay?" I asked as they climbed out of Luke's truck.

"Luke made sure everyone made it home safe and sound," Elva assured me. "The gang wanted to meet tonight, but Luke talked them into waiting until tomorrow."

I glanced at Luke. He shrugged.

"We're meeting tomorrow?" I asked.

"Emmy Jean thought we should get the gang back together," Elva explained, referring to one half of the sister duo— with Tammy Rhea—I thought of as the Southern sisters. "She reminded us how much we helped you and Luke track down Stuart Bronson's killer last summer."

"That's true, you all did help, but I'm not sure Luke and I will be investigating Sam's murder."

"Not investigate?" Elva appeared to be scandalized. "You have to. Sam was our friend and he was doing you a favor when he was murdered. The way we see it, it's your responsibility to find his killer."

I didn't disagree with Elva, but Jason wasn't going to like it if I got involved.

"Tell her, Luke." Elva turned to the man who had to that point been standing silently in the background. "Tell Lani it's important that we pull together to figure this whole thing out."

"Perhaps Lani and I should talk things through," Luke suggested. "We already have plans with the others to meet at my house for lunch tomorrow. I suggest we see one another then and take things from there. For all we know, HPD will have made an arrest by then and our help won't be needed."

There was a look of uncertainty on Elva's face as she turned back to me. "Okay," she eventually agreed. "We can talk about it tomorrow at lunch. I'm going to head in. It's been a long day."

"Good night, Elva." I hugged my neighbor. "And don't worry. We'll make sure Sam's killer is brought to justice one way or another."

After Elva went inside I grabbed my dog, Sandy, and Luke and we went for a walk on the beach. It had been a very long day at the end of a very long week, but at least I had the next two days off. Before I'd left the resort for the evening Kekoa had informed me that resort management had decided to honor everyone's set days off and had hired a temp agency to help out through the holidays.

"Are you okay?" Luke asked as he took my hand.

"Not really. I just can't believe someone killed kind, sweet Sam. Who would do such a thing?"

"I don't know."

I rested my head on Luke's shoulder as a wave lapped up onto the shore and covered our bare feet. It was a clear night with a sky full of stars that at any other time I would have found romantic, but tonight I found it haunting.

"Do you think it's a good idea to get the seniors involved in this?" I asked.

"Not at all. The problem is that they're already involved. They were all friends of Sam's and they were all at the party while he was murdered. I tried to calm everyone down while I was taking them home, but I wasn't having much success. When Emmy Jean suggested getting the sleuthing gang back together everyone agreed."

"I know they helped with Stuart's murder investigation, but I don't want anyone getting hurt."

"Which is why I suggested lunch tomorrow. Last summer, when they were all fired up to help out, I think we did a good job letting them be involved without actually having them in any danger. We agreed then that allowing them to participate in a controlled environment was a better idea than taking the chance they'd go off on their own."

I stopped walking and looked out at the dark sea. "You're right. I'm just tired and the whole thing seems overwhelming, but I guess lunch is a good idea. If we give them a forum to express their feelings and offer suggestions, they'll feel they're contributing and probably are less likely to go off on their own. At least I hope that's what happens. There's still the possibility that the whole thing could backfire and someone really will end up getting hurt."

"Maybe Jason will find the killer right away and none of this will be necessary."

"Here's hoping that's what happens." I leaned my body into Luke's for both comfort and support as the waves lapped onto the shore.

"How about we go to my place and I make you a late supper?" Luke suggested.

"I'm not really hungry."

"I'll make my special grilled cheese."

I smiled at the wonderful man I was lucky to have in my life. "Grilled cheese sounds perfect. Do you have potato chips?"

"Of course. I always keep your favorite brand on hand. Bring whatever you need to stay over. We'll have sandwiches and then get a good night's sleep. Tomorrow is soon enough to tackle whatever comes next."

Chapter 3

Sunday, December 18

Unfortunately, HPD hadn't solved the mystery of who'd murdered Sam Riverton by the time the seniors arrived at Luke's house the following day. Luke made a seafood salad that, combined with crusty bread, was a perfect midday meal. The warm weather was holding, so we set up a table outside near the pool and waterfall. Luke had the perfect patio for entertaining. There were both covered and uncovered places to sit and the pool, combined with lush foliage, made the perfect setting for an outdoor kitchen.

"Where's Emmy Jean? She's the one who suggested this lunch in the first place," Janice complained.

"She called to tell me Tammy Rhea had a salon appointment so they'd be a few minutes late," Luke explained.

"Tammy Rhea goes to the salon more often than anyone I've ever known," Beth

Wasserman, the most athletic of the group, commented.

"I say we start without the Southern sisters if they can't get here on time," Elva asserted. "We've got a lot to go over and as far as I'm concerned, the sooner we track down Sam's killer the better."

"Does anyone know if any of the others are coming?" Janice asked.

"I believe it's just the three of you, Emmy Jean and Tammy Rhea, Lani and me," Luke answered.

"Tammy Rhea isn't even a permanent member of the senior group," Beth grumbled. "I'm not sure why we need to include her just because she happens to be visiting her sister."

"She does talk a lot, diverting all the attention away from the subject at hand," Janice agreed. "In fact, neither sister brings much to the table, if you ask me."

I suspected Janice was simply jealous of the Southern sisters, who were both outgoing and just a bit outrageous. Janice had been single for quite a few years and had never shown any interest in dating until a year ago, when she'd announced out of the blue that she wanted to get remarried and had joined a dating service. The main problem I saw with Janice's plan was that she was seventy-five and had put an upper age limit on the men she would date at fifty-five. Janice said she wanted a companion to have fun with during her final years, not an old man she'd need to nurse should his health fail.

"Both Emmy Jean and Tammy Rhea helped quite a bit last summer," I reminded her. "Besides, it would be rude to exclude them. I'm sure they'll be along shortly."

Janice shot me a dirty look but didn't reply.

"Lani and I are going to head back into the kitchen to grab the sweet tea and lemonade. Why don't you ladies go ahead and take seats at the table we set up in the shade?" Luke said.

"Do you have regular tea also?" Beth asked. "I'm trying to watch my weight."

I rolled my eyes. Of all the seniors, Beth was the only one who didn't need to count calories. She both taught yoga and participated in triathlons on a regular basis.

"I'll bring out regular tea as well," Luke promised as he took my hand and led me to the kitchen.

"I think I'm going to check in with Jason one more time before we sit down to eat," I informed him.

"That might be a good idea. If nothing else you can let him know the seniors are stirred up and ready to tackle this investigation on their own if need be."

"Yeah, he's going to love that," I said sarcastically.

I sat down at the kitchen counter and called my brother. I knew he was probably over-the-top busy, but I knew he'd want a heads-up that the seniors were on the warpath. "Hey, Jason, just checking in. Any news?"

"Not really. We have a few leads we're looking in to, but I doubt they'll pan out."

"Did you ever get hold of Titan?"

"Yeah. We tracked him down at the resort this morning."

"Did you ask him about the missing footage?"

"He said he didn't know anything about it. He claims he went into his office to check his emails before he left for the day and that was what the guard on duty must have noticed. At this point we don't have anything to indicate that he's lying, but we're taking a close look at the video feed, so maybe we'll come up with something. Our tech guy did say it looked like the feed had been altered from a remote server, and if that's true, he most likely wasn't the one who did it."

"I hope he turns out to be innocent. He's worked at the resort for a long time and he's a really nice guy."

I listened as Jason paused to speak to someone else. It was noisy in the background, so Jason was probably juggling more than one crime at a time.

"I need to go. It's crazy around here this morning," Jason said, confirming my suspicion.

"Okay, but before you do, I think you should know that some of the seniors who were at the party last night showed up at Luke's and seem determined to launch their own investigation."

I heard Jason let out a sigh of frustration. "That's the last thing we need."

"I know. I agree. I don't think either of us wants them to put themselves in danger. Luke suggested we join them in their efforts so we can keep an eye on the situation."

"I don't want you to put yourself in danger either."

"I can use good judgment," I defended myself.

Jason didn't answer.

"Look, the seniors want to be involved and if we don't support them, they'll do it on their own."

"I guess you have a point. But keep me in the loop at all times, and whatever you do, you're to avoid confrontation or dangerous situations. If you get a lead call me and I'll follow up."

"I will. I promise. I'll snoop safely from the sidelines."

"I'll call you later. And Lani, I mean it. Be careful."

After I hung up I filled Luke in on the conversation.

"I have a feeling this case is going to be more than just a little bit complicated. Grab the lemonade and I'll get both types of tea," Luke instructed. "We'd best get back before our guests get restless."

By the time we returned to the patio Emmy Jean and Tammy Rhea had arrived. Tammy Rhea, who previously had had red hair, now sported a bright purple do. Both Emmy Jean and Tammy Rhea were the flamboyant sort, with big hair, big boobs, tons of makeup, and clothing so tight I couldn't imagine how anyone could sit in it.

"Did you see Tammy Rhea's hair?" Emmy Jean asked.

"Yes," I answered. "It's very colorful."

"We went down to one of those fancy salons in Waikiki and Tammy Rhea had a signature color mixed up. The girl assured us it's a custom color that was created to support her specific coloring and taste. I'm thinking about having mine done next week."

I smiled in response. The color was pretty horrible. And to make matters worse, Tammy Rhea wore a bright, peach-colored lipstick that caused her naturally pale skin to take on an orangish hue.

"And what color are you thinking of getting?" Elva asked Emmy Jean.

"I'm not totally sure. At first I was thinking orange, but I like the red Tammy Rhea has on her toes. Tammy Rhea, show everyone your toes."

Tammy Rhea slipped off one of her shoes and wiggled her toes in front of everyone.

"I think we've discussed hair and nails long enough," Janice interrupted. "Let's get down to business. We're gathered here today for one purpose and one purpose only: to track down and bring to justice the man or woman who killed poor, sweet Sam."

"Janice is right," Beth agreed. "It isn't sitting well with me at all that Sam is dead and the killer is still on the loose."

"I guess the obvious place to start is to try to determine who might have wanted Sam dead," I contributed. "You knew him as well as anyone, Beth; did he have any enemies you know of?"

The group became quiet. I supposed they must be taking a moment to contemplate their answers.

"Janice wasn't too happy when Sam asked me to attend the senior social with him," Emmy Jean pointed out. "Talk about a jealous rage. Woo-wee, if looks could kill Sam would have been dead weeks ago."

"I didn't kill Sam," Janice insisted. "And I didn't send him any dirty looks. Sam and I were just friends. He was free to date whoever he wanted."

"Friends my ass. I know you were jealous of the fact that Sam wanted to spend time with me when it was clear as day you had your sights on him. Admit it; you had it bad for him."

"Don't be ridiculous," Janice scoffed. "Sam was sixty-six years old, which is a good eleven years out of my desired age range."

"Maybe, but I saw the way you looked at him. The way your eyes lit up when he came into a room. You were in love with the man and he never even noticed. I could see the jealousy in your eyes every time the two of us were together."

"Even if Janice was jealous—and I'm not saying she was," I glanced at both

Janice and Emmy Jean, "she was sitting at the table with you when Sam was killed, so she couldn't have done it."

"I guess that's true," Emmy Jean was forced to admit.

"What about Brock Littleton?" Beth suggested.

"Who's Brock Littleton?" I asked.

"Brock Littleton is, or I guess I should say was, Sam's neighbor," Elva answered. "Sam and Brock had a falling out a while back over an apple tree that, while planted on Sam's property, hung over the fence and dropped apples onto Brock's property."

"I very much doubt someone would kill a man over a few apples," I countered.

"I don't know," Janice jumped in. "Brock was pretty mad. He's sort of OCD and he didn't appreciate the fact that Sam's tree was littering his yard. Sam said he even threatened to take him to small claims court if Sam didn't trim back the tree."

"Why didn't Sam do it?" I wondered.

"He was getting back at Brock for the music," Beth answered.

"Music?" I asked.

"Brock likes opera and he plays his stereo quite loud. Sam hated opera. He used to say it sounded like a cat in a blender and was about to drive him totally over the edge. He even talked about breaking into Brock's house when he wasn't home and destroying his stereo, but Emmy Jean pointed out to him that he'd not only buy a new one but probably retaliate by playing the music even louder."

"Even if Brock was mad enough about the apples to kill Sam, there's no way he could have known he'd be at the resort last night," Luke pointed out.

"True," Janice said. "The Santa gig was a last-minute thing."

"We need to figure out who had a problem with Sam and knew where to find him last night," I added.

"Sam's brother Steven was at the senior center when you called to ask Sam to fill in," Emmy Jean provided.

"And were Sam and Steven having issues in their relationship?" I asked.

"Steven is the irresponsible type who can't hold a job and is always getting into one scrape or another, even though he's almost sixty. Anyway, their mother died a few months ago after a long illness. Their father passed away several years before that, so Sam and Steven were the only heirs to their parents' estate. At one point the brothers were told that when the last of them died the estate would be divided equally between the brothers, but when the mother's will was read it turned out she'd left everything to Sam, with instructions for him to use a portion of the money to take care of his brother's basic expenses so he wouldn't end up on the street. It appears that didn't go over too well with either of them. Steven wanted his half of the money and Sam didn't want to have to babysit his brother for the rest of his life. According to Sam, the will created a rift between them, particularly when it became obvious that Steven's definition of *basic expenses* were quite different from his brother's. I don't know if Steven was mad enough over the whole thing to kill Sam, but he was definitely giving him the cold shoulder on the day he died."

"I wonder if Steven gets the money now that Sam's dead," I mused.

"It would be worth our time to look in to it," Luke voiced.

I took out my phone and started a list on it. I wrote down Steven's name.

"As long as you're making a list, you may as well add Sam's ex," Janice added.

"Sam had an ex?" I asked. "I thought he was a widower."

"He was," Janice confirmed. "He married his high school sweetheart as soon as he graduated from college. They were married for twenty years but eventually divorced. Then he met and married his second wife, who passed away a couple of years ago."

"And wife number one is still in the picture?" Luke asked.

"Apparently," Janice said. "She never remarried, so Sam had been paying her alimony all those years. He mentioned to me one Monday when we both arrived early for bingo that she felt she should have gotten a percentage of his mother's estate. She was entitled to a percentage of his income and she considered the inheritance to be income."

"That doesn't seem right," I commented.

Janice shrugged. "I really don't know the terms of his divorce, but Sam was worried about the lawsuit his ex-wife was threatening to initiate if they couldn't come to an understanding."

"Yeah, but with Sam dead she wouldn't have any case," I pointed out. "It really doesn't seem like his ex would have motive to kill him."

"Maybe not, but she knew where Sam was going to be last night. He mentioned to me that he needed to stop by her place to pick up the Santa suit, which she'd borrowed for a charity event."

"I'll add her to the list. Do you know her name?" I asked Janice.

"Beatrice Riverton. She's a volunteer over at the library."

"You know, you should put some colored lights on that palm near the waterfall," Tammy Rhea suddenly commented. It seemed obvious she was bored with all the murder talk.

"That would look nice," Emmy Jean seconded. "And I saw some of those reindeer that have white lights on them over at the hardware store that would really brighten up the patio area. It's only a week until Christmas, you know. I didn't even notice a tree in your living room when I popped in to use the ladies' room."

"Luke was in Texas visiting his family until a few days ago," I reminded the group.

"Maybe, but he's back now," Tammy Rhea insisted. "Do you have lights and such?"

"Actually I don't," Luke answered.

Tammy Rhea made a sound in her throat that demonstrated her displeasure. "I bet your mama would have a fit if she could see your place."

"You've never even met Luke's mama," Beth said gently. "How would you know whether she would have a fit about the lack of decorations?"

"She's Southern born and bred and we Southerners like to do the holidays up right." Tammy Rhea turned to Luke. "How about you and I go buy what we need and then we'll all help you decorate this afternoon?"

"Decorate?" Janice asked. "I thought we were going to investigate."

"I agree with Janice," Elva jumped in. "Lights would look nice, but we need to find Sam's killer."

"Why don't we split up?" Emmy Jean said instead. "Tammy Rhea and I will go with Luke to get the decorations while Lani, Elva, Janice, and Beth follow up with the suspects we've identified. We'll all meet back here later and Luke can cook us up some steaks for supper."

Luke glanced at me with a look that said *help*, while I tried to think of a way around Emmy Jean's plan. We could tell her that we had plans for the evening, but she wasn't likely to take no for an answer.

"Luke really should be the one to talk to Sam's brother," I tried. "In fact, he'd probably do best with Brock as well. Why don't Luke and I follow up on our leads while the rest of you go with Emmy Jean in her car to buy the decorations? We'll all meet back here for a BBQ and we can fill you in on what we found."

"I guess that would be okay," Emmy Jean agreed.

Luckily, the others agreed as well.

Chapter 4

"I'm not sure how wise it was to leave the ladies unsupervised," I admitted as Luke and I drove to the address we'd be given for Steven. "You might come home to pink flamingos wearing holiday wreaths with purple flashing lights."

"That's okay. The gals were right; I could use some holiday trimmings, and despite their choice in hair color, I'm willing to bet the Southern sisters have a flare for decorating. Should I turn left or right ahead?"

"Left."

Luke slowed as he approached the intersection. "I don't mind taking the time to have a chat with Steven, but I think it's pretty unlikely he had anything to do with Sam's death. Even if Steven did know Sam would be at the resort last night, how could he possibly have known he'd be in the alley at that time?"

"I agree with you. I don't think Steven is a likely suspect, but he might know something about Sam that only a family member would. Besides, the seniors aren't going to be content to sit on the sidelines unless we're actively investigating. Making sure they don't go off and do something that will get them hurt has to be our main priority."

"Which house is it?"

"The house number is 1620, so it must be the yellow one on the left with the brick wall."

Luke pulled up in front of the house. He cut the engine and we both took a moment to gather our thoughts before heading up to the front door. I'd called Steven prior to our visit. I didn't know him well, but I had seen him a time or two at the senior center. We decided on the approach we would use, then headed to the front door and rang the bell.

"Lani, how are you?" Steven greeted me.

"I'm fine, thank you. I'm so sorry about your brother."

"It's been quite a shock. Please come in." We followed him inside and took seats on the sofa. "How can I help you?"

"I guess you heard I was the one who asked Sam to fill in for Santa, and I was also the one who found him."

"Yes, I heard."

"Some of the senior women who were at the party last night have asked us to help them make sense of what happened. We're visiting those closest to Sam in the hope that we might be able to better understand what was going on in his life prior to his death."

"You're looking for a motive?"

I glanced at Luke. He shrugged. "I guess that's one way to put it."

Steven sat forward and looked me in the eye. "Just so we're clear on this, I can assure you I didn't kill my brother. Sam and I had our differences, but I loved and even respected him. To be honest, Sam looked out for me. I'm not sure what I'm going to do now that he's gone."

"I understand he helped you out financially."

"In a roundabout way." Steven briefly explained the terms of his mother's will. "I was pretty mad at first. I'm almost sixty years old. I certainly don't need a babysitter. But after I'd had a chance to gain some perspective I could see that maybe she was wise to do what she did. When the will was read I felt betrayed that she didn't leave me the money directly, but now that Sam's gone and the money is mine, I'm at a loss for what to do with it. Sam always was better at that kind of thing."

"There are people who can help you with that," Luke offered. "Good people you can trust. I can give you some names if you'd like."

"Thank you. That might be a good idea."

I rested my arms on my knees. "I'm sure you knew Sam better than anyone else. Can you think of anyone who would want him dead?"

"Offhand I can't think of a single person. Sam was a nice guy. People liked and respected him. He looked out for the well-being of others."

"So there was no one he had a quarrel with?"

Steven frowned. "Not really. Sam was a sociable guy, well liked and popular. He had a lot of friends and belonged to quite a few groups and organizations. I know he did a lot of volunteer work."

"Volunteer work?" I asked.

"He helped out with a reading program the school down the street sponsored a couple of days a week and served meals at the soup kitchen the church a couple of blocks over operates on Mondays and Thursdays."

I made a note of the name of the church as well as the school. Steven didn't have the name of a contact for either program, but I could just ask at the front desk.

"Anything else you can thing of?"

"That's all I know for certain. Sam spent quite a bit of time at the senior center and I know he dated several women. I think his catting around probably led to a few broken hearts, but I'm not sure who exactly he might have hurt. He wasn't one to kiss and tell."

"What about his ex-wife, Beatrice?"

"Bea wouldn't kill Sam. Bea loved Sam. Always had and always will."

"I heard she'd been threatening him with a lawsuit."

"Threats were just her way of flirting."

"Come again?"

"When Sam left Bea she was crushed. For reasons I still don't understand, he decided he no longer wanted to be married to her, but she was still very much in love with him. After he left she began to create reasons to spend time with him. They'd never had children, so she didn't have that to keep him in her life, but that didn't stop Bea. At first she managed to hang on by asking for help with home repairs or suddenly finding something he thought he'd lost in an old box of her stuff. When Sam told her he was going to remarry she became desperate and begged him to continue to take care of her. I wasn't privy to all the details, but I will say Bea spent a lot of time and money ensuring that he'd continue to be a part of her life."

"What do you mean by time and money?"

"Like this lawsuit to try to get some of Mother's estate. She had no hope of winning. And based on what I overheard she knew it. But threatening to sue Sam gave her a reason to meet with him, talk with him, try to find a middle ground. Personally, I don't know why Bea tried so hard with Sam. She's a lovely person who could have done better. Sam never appreciated her the way he should have. I tried to tell her that she should move on and find someone worthy of her, but she wouldn't listen."

It didn't sound like either Steven or Beatrice were going to turn out to be credible suspects. If we couldn't nail down a motive perhaps we'd be better off trying for opportunity. "I know Sam was at the senior center when I called him about the Santa gig. I also know there were quite a few people around who overheard the conversation I had with him and would know he was going to be at the resort last night."

"Yes, that's true. Sam was excited at the opportunity and made a big announcement that he'd be playing Santa at the Step into Christmas party. I can try to make you a list of who was around if that will help."

"Thank you. That would help quite a lot."

Steven got a pen and a notepad from the desk and began to jot down names as we spoke. I'd ask the ladies who were at the senior center with Sam when I called to make their own list; perhaps among them all we'd have a complete accounting.

"Sam was offered a table for eight as a thank-you for filling in for Santa. I know he invited seven people who were with him at the time I called him to be his guests. I'm wondering why he didn't ask you."

"He did. I didn't want to go. Those fancy parties aren't for me, and to be honest, I thought it was strange that he wanted to dress up like the jolly old man in the first place. I'd be embarrassed to get all dressed up like that, but Sam seemed to enjoy it."

"If you didn't go to the party with the others from the senior center where were you last night?"

"At the resort."

I frowned.

"One of the guys wanted to take a video of Sam all dressed up in his furry red outfit to post to a senior chat room where Sam likes to socialize. We'd had a few drinks and thought the video would embarrass Sam, but looking back, he wouldn't have been embarrassed at all. He was really into the gig."

"Who were you with at the resort?"

"Walt Goodman, Ted Browning, and Gil Portland."

"And did you get your video?"

"No. We missed him. We saw you take him to the locker room to change, but we got thirsty and tired of waiting, so we headed to the beach bar instead."

"And were the four of you together the entire time?"

"Mostly. I mean, Walt had to use the can and the rest of us didn't follow him there, and Ted had to call his wife, so he went outside where it wasn't so loud. I went outside to smoke and the others didn't follow me, and Gil went outside for some fresh air at one point, but it didn't seem like he was gone long." Steven frowned and looked directly at me. "You don't think one of the guys killed Sam, do you?"

"I don't know. Do you?"

Steven didn't answer, but I could see he was considering the likelihood that one of the guys had done just that.

"Did any of the men you were with have a reason to want Sam out of the way?" I asked.

Steven narrowed his eyes. "I hate to say anything and throw an innocent man under the bus, but yeah, one of them had a beef with my brother. It seems Sam may have made a move on one of the women who volunteers at the soup kitchen. Her name is Tina. I don't know her last name. Tina and Walt used to date before Sam started coming around there. Now that I think about it, it was Walt's idea to follow Sam to the resort in the first place."

"Do you know where we can find him?"

"He lives over near Waialee. I don't have his address, but I'm sure the guy who runs the soup kitchen can tell you. I know they keep records on their volunteers."

"I'll follow up," I assured Steven.

He handed me the piece of notepaper on which he'd been writing names down. "That's all I can remember offhand."

"Thank you. This is helpful. Again, I'm very sorry for your loss."

Luke and I headed back to the car.

"What do you think?" I asked.

"I think it might be worth our while to speak to both Walt and Tina. But we don't have contact info, so I guess we should start with the church where the soup kitchen is held."

We drove to the community church, which served neighbors of all denominations. The minister told us the man who ran the soup kitchen was a volunteer named Joshua Simon. The minister was fairly certain we could find him today at the community center, where he coached youth basketball.

"Boy, does this bring back memories," Luke said as we walked into the large building where bleachers full of spectators were watching a group of kids who looked to be around eleven or twelve running up and down the court.

"Did you play when you were a kid?"

"All the way through high school and into college."

That made sense. Luke was tall. And athletic. And oh so sexy. I could almost picture him dripping with sweat as he ran up and down the court in shorts and a basketball jersey that showed off his tan legs and muscular arms. As I felt my face flush, I realized I'd better get my mind out of the bedroom and back on the murder.

"I'll just ask someone to point out Joshua Simon," I said. "If he's one of the coaches in the middle of a game I hope it'll be over soon."

"They're only halfway through the first quarter," Luke informed me.

"Quarter as in four time periods exactly like this one?"

"Yes."

That figured. If he was on the court we'd either have to wait for him to be done or try to speak to him another day. As it turned out, Joshua Simon was in the middle of the game, but Luke seemed to be enjoying watching, so we elected to stay until it was over. Basketball wasn't my favorite game to watch. It basically consisted of nothing more than a group of people running back and forth from one end of the court to the other trying to toss a round ball through a round hoop. There was a certain element of competition that appealed to me, but there were several other sports I'd rather watch if given the choice.

"Isn't this fun?" Luke asked.

"Yeah. Fun."

"It's been quite a while since I played, but now that I know this place is here I might check to see if they have an adult league."

I looked at Luke as he remained riveted on the game. It was times like this that brought home to me how different he and I were.

"Great game," Luke said, shaking Joshua Simon's hand when it finally ended. "Your starting point guard is really something."

"Yeah, he has a promising career ahead of him if he can stay focused and keep his head in the game. So, how can I help you?"

Luke explained. It was evident he and the tall man he was chatting with had bonded over this ridiculous game, so I was happy to let him take the lead.

"Sam is dead?" Simon gasped.

"It happened last night," Luke told him.

He shook his head. It was obvious he was truly grieved. "I just saw him on Thursday. I can't believe he's gone."

"How did you think he was when you saw him last?" I asked. "Did he seem nervous or worried?"

Simon paused. "No. He seemed fine. He'd found some local sponsors to donate food to the soup kitchen so we could serve a huge holiday meal to anyone who wanted to come by. We mostly cater to the least fortunate, but when it comes to the holidays there are those who might be able to afford a meal but don't have anyone to share the day with. Serving a community-wide feast open to everyone regardless of income was Sam's idea."

"It sounds like he was a good man," Luke commented.

"One of the best."

"Did he seem to have any conflicts with either the other volunteers or the people you served each week?" I asked.

Simon shook his head. "No. Everyone loved Sam. I can't think of a single person who would have anything bad to say about him."

"I understand you also have a volunteer named Walt Goodman," I offered.

"We do."

"We have reason to believe Walt was with Sam on the night he died. We'd like to speak to him to find out what he might remember. We were hoping you could provide us with his contact information."

"I'd love to help you track down Sam's killer, but I'm afraid I can't give out personal information that's been provided by our volunteers."

"I guess I can understand that. I don't suppose you know when Walt is due to be in the soup kitchen next?"

"Walt volunteers on Mondays. If you happened to stop by tomorrow in the late afternoon I'm fairly certain he'll be at the church."

"Thank you." I smiled at Simon. "We will stop by. Sam was a friend and we're committed to finding out who ended his life. If you think of anything—anything at all that might help us figure out what might have happened—please call me."

I handed the man a paper with my cell number on it.

He turned to Luke. "There is something I can't make up my mind about mentioning. It seems it might be sort of delicate."

"We can be discreet," Luke assured him. "We just want to find Sam's killer."

Simon still looked uncertain, but he must have decided to trust us because he began to speak. "You might want to talk to a man named Ray Clark. He used to volunteer at the soup kitchen along with Sam, but they had a falling-out and I haven't seen Ray since. I'm not saying I think Ray would kill anyone. Quite the contrary; Ray is a good man."

"Do you know what the falling-out was about?" I asked.

"I don't have any details, but it seemed Ray found out something about Sam that didn't sit quite right. I don't know what it was, but the two argued and then Ray stopped coming around. It was a shame really."

"And when was the last time you saw Ray?" I asked.

Simon bit his lip and rolled his eyes as he seemed to search his memory. "It must have been a month ago, maybe six weeks. I don't remember exactly. It was a shame to lose him as a volunteer. He was a hard worker and the regulars liked him."

"I don't suppose you can provide a phone number or address for Clark either?"

"No, I'm afraid I can't."

I thanked Simon and Luke and I headed back to his truck.

"Why does that name sound familiar?" Luke asked.

I paused next to the passenger door as I waited for Luke to unlock the vehicle. "It's not ringing a bell with me. Although now that you mention it, it does sort of seem familiar. Maybe the seniors will know who he is."

Chapter 5

By the time we got back to Luke's the sun had set. As we turned off the main highway onto the country road that led to Luke's ranch, a bright light became visible in the distance.

I laughed. "How much do you want to bet that beacon in the dark is your house?"

Luke chuckled in return. "I guess it's a good thing I don't have any close neighbors."

"I hope the bright lights don't spook the horses."

"If there are any lights shining into the barn or pasture area I'll adjust them." Luke pulled onto the dirt drive leading to his house just as the Santa and six reindeer that had been secured to the roof came on.

"How in the world did the gals get that up there?" I asked in amazement.

Luke didn't answer, but I could see his face held the same look of confusion as my own. When we pulled up to the house and saw Brody Weller, a fellow WSO who lived in Luke's guest house, climbing down a ladder we had our answer.

"Why didn't you warn me about the senior decorating crew?" Brody whispered after we parked and got out of the truck. "I came over to the house to borrow one of your beers and ended up climbing ladders all afternoon."

"That's what you get for not buying your own beer," Luke teased.

"You can be sure the next time I will. Heck of a way to spend a day off."

"Helping the seniors didn't kill you and the house does look nice," I commented as I stood back and took in the white lights that weren't only strung along the eaves of the large house but were draped over much of the shrubbery as well. "It feels like Santa's village."

"Santa's village has snow," Brody said.

"True. But it's beautiful, although I would like to have a white Christmas one day."

"Maybe next Christmas we can go to Texas to visit my family." Luke took my hand in his.

"You have snow for Christmas in Texas?"

"Not everywhere and not every year, but in the Panhandle, where my family lives, we've been known to have a white Christmas from time to time."

Christmas in Texas. The thought both thrilled and terrified me.

"Luke, Lani, I'm so glad y'all are back. What do you think?" Emmy Jean called out.

"It's beautiful," I responded.

"Feels a lot like home," Luke seconded.

"Wait until you see the patio." Emmy Jean took Luke's hand and started down the pathway that led from the front of the house around to the patio in the back while I followed behind. The decorating team had lined the pathway with red and green lights, making it easy to navigate in the dark.

"Wow," I said as we rounded the corner and the deck came into sight.

"Wow is right," Luke agreed.

The women had strategically placed illuminated animals among the foliage, making for a magical outdoor garden. The bear cubs were adorable, but my favorite was the penguin that had been placed so it appeared as if he was sliding down the waterfall toward the pool.

"We thought we'd eat out on the patio," Tammy Rhea joined in. "It might get a little chilly, but you have those overhead heaters in the covered area, so I'm sure we'll be toasty warm. You did bring the steaks?"

Luke held up the grocery bag in his hand. "Steaks, Texas beans, salad, and grilled sourdough bread."

"Sounds perfect." Tammy Rhea smiled. "I do love Texas beans. I remember one time my mama…"

"This has been fun and all," Janice interrupted, "but we gathered in the first place to discuss Sam's murder. Do you have any news?"

"Some," I answered. "I'm starving. Why don't we get dinner on the table and then we can talk while we eat?"

"I take it you haven't found the killer," Janice concluded. "If you had you would have come right out and said so."

"No, we haven't found the killer, but we did pick up some new leads. I think between all of us we can come up with a plan for tomorrow. Would you like to help me with the salad while Luke gets the steaks on the grill?"

Janice shrugged but followed me inside.

While it was apparent the ladies had spent most of their time outdoors, there were a few holiday lights strung indoors as well. While my family always had a fake Christmas tree growing up, Cam, Kekoa, and I hadn't bothered with one at all since we'd moved in together, mostly due to limited space. Luke had a huge great room with a vaulted ceiling and I knew a tree, maybe the Norfolk pines some of the people I knew favored, would look spectacular in front of the window. Maybe I'd suggest a trip to the local Christmas tree farm the following day.

"Why don't you chop some lettuce while I slice the tomatoes?" I suggested to Janice. "There's a bowl in the cupboard to the left."

Janice reached for the bowl and began to chop.

"The house sure does look nice," I complimented. "You all did a wonderful job."

"It does look nice and I did have a pleasant time helping out, but I'm worried that we're getting distracted from our original purpose. It seems between all the decorating and talk of a Christmas potluck tomorrow afternoon, everyone has forgotten about tracking down Sam's killer."

"Christmas potluck?" I asked.

"Elva brought it up. She thinks that because tomorrow is the last Monday before Christmas we should skip our weekly lunch and have a potluck at bingo."

"Sounds like fun."

"Maybe, but it's still a distraction."

I stopped what I was doing and looked directly at Janice. "I think people deal with grief differently. Emmy Jean and Tammy Rhea dealt with their grief by decorating and Elva dealt with hers by planning a party."

"Is that why Beth did about a hundred laps in Luke's pool after you left?"

"Probably."

Janice scooped the lettuce she'd chopped into a bowl and started in on a cucumber. "Well, I want to deal with my grief by finding Sam's killer. I'd known him the longest; maybe that's why I feel more of an urgency than the others, but all this sitting around doing nothing is driving me crazy."

"How long *had* you known Sam?" I asked.

"More than ten years. I was friends with his second wife, Hester, and after she passed I began helping out by taking Sam a casserole a couple of times a week. After he'd worked through his grief a bit I invited him to join the senior center."

"I wasn't aware you knew him before he joined the center." I arranged the sliced tomatoes in the bowl and began to slice some olives.

"Well, I did. Sam and I have been through a lot together. We were the best of friends until Emmy Jean came along and ruined what we had."

"Were you dating?"

"No. Not dating. But we did hang out together. I knew Sam had girlfriends—heck, half the women at the center have dated and been dumped by Sam—but I didn't mind. None of them lasted long and I really wasn't interested in having that sort of relationship with him. When Emmy Jean joined the senior center I could see he was drawn to her. I expected he'd move on after a couple of dates, but he didn't."

I used a knife to slide the olives from the cutting board into the salad bowl. "Did it bother you that Sam and Emmy Jean seemed to have developed a real relationship?"

"Of course it bothered me. Not in the way you think; I wasn't in love with Sam and I didn't look at him as a potential sexual companion, but I liked spending time with him and Emmy Jean's presence felt like an intrusion."

I'd had no idea Janice had felt that way about Sam. She wasn't one to overshare, but you would think I would have picked up on the fact that Sam and Janice were that close. Emmy Jean had suggested that Sam and Janice had a close relationship;

now I wondered if the others had realized it too. It was probable Emmy Jean had taken Tammy Rhea into her confidence. They were sisters and they seemed to be close. This was the third time Tammy Rhea had visited this year that I knew of. It wouldn't surprise me if she didn't end up moving to Oahu before too long.

"Because you've known Sam the longest, is there anything you know about his past that might help explain why he was murdered?"

"We've already discussed Sam's brother and ex. Both make viable suspects in my mind. I don't really know what arrangements were made for the money Sam inherited from his mother, but it seems likely it will go to Steven now."

"Luke and I spoke to Steven today. He admitted to being at the resort last night, but I didn't pick up on any vibes that he'd murdered him. He seemed to be genuinely lost and grieving."

"If not Steven, how about Beatrice? Hester never had a nice thing to say about her. I never met her, but from what I've heard she sounds like a nutcase."

"While we haven't spoken to Beatrice, Steven seemed certain she was still in love with Sam and would never have killed him."

"I don't know Steven well, but in my opinion he isn't the sort of person who should necessarily be believed or trusted. And even if Beatrice was still in love with Sam, we both know love can make you do wacky things, especially when it's unrequited."

I sliced some bread and began to butter it while Janice mixed up the salad dressing. "I suppose you have a point. I'll see what I can find out about Beatrice. Did you know about Sam's volunteer work?"

"Yes, I knew. He got involved in a lot of different things after Hester died. I don't think he liked being alone with his memories. He seemed to love her quite a lot."

"How did she die?"

"In an auto accident. It was a hit and run and they never did track down the guilty party. I know that haunted Sam. He told me losing your soul mate is the worst thing anyone can experience, but never having a resolution for the loss makes things even harder. Maybe that's why I'm so impatient to solve Sam's murder. I know how much finding justice for an innocent victim meant to him."

I stopped what I was doing and gave Janice a hug. Unlike most of the seniors, who welcomed a warm embrace, Janice wasn't the hugging sort, but on this occasion she didn't pull away.

"We'll figure out who did this," I promised. "Let's go enjoy this wonderful dinner and then we'll come up with a plan."

After everyone had served themselves the group settled around the large table Luke had moved near the outdoor fireplace. Snow would be awesome, but Luke's patio with the decorations and cozy fire felt like a pretty magical place as it was.

I filled the group in on the little Luke and I had found out while we ate. "We may not have eliminated any of our suspects, but we did get a new lead: Ray Clark."

"I hadn't thought about speaking to Ray, but now that his name has been brought up I think interviewing him is a wonderful idea," Janice said.

"You know Ray?" I asked.

"Sort of. He used to volunteer with Sam and they became good friends. I don't know him well, but I've met him a time or two. I haven't actually seen him for quite a while. I'm not sure what happened, but he and Sam had a falling out a while back and Ray stopped coming around."

"I thought the name sounded familiar, but I can't quite place him," Luke commented.

Janice set down her fork. "That's because you probably know him as RJ Clark."

"The local news anchor?"

"That would be him," Janice answered Luke.

"It seems like an odd pairing. Sam must have been a good twenty years older than RJ," I said.

"Sam had a way about him that appealed to people of all ages," Janice explained. "You should have seen him with the kids in the reading program where he volunteered. He knew how to engage them with his jokes and stories." A sad look came over Janice's face. "I'm really going to miss him."

"I'm sorry I gave you a hard time before," Emmy Jean offered. "Sam was a special man and I know we're all going to miss having him in our lives."

"So what do we do now?" Beth asked.

"We need to look not only at motive but opportunity," I told the others. "Between the five of you and Steven we have what should be a good list of who was at the senior center at the time I called to ask Sam to fill in as Santa. Whoever killed

Sam would not only need to have a motive but would also have to have the knowledge that Sam was at the resort that evening. Steven has already admitted to being there with Walt Goodman, Ted Browning, and Gil Portland."

"And there were the seven of us who were Sam's guests," Elva added.

"Susan left early, but were the rest of you together the entire time?" I asked.

"Surely you don't think one of us killed Sam?" Tammy Rhea looked and sounded scandalized.

"No. Of course I don't think one of you killed Sam. But I've found when taking part in an investigation it's important to be as thorough as possible."

"We arrived with Sam at a little before five," Beth began. "The party wasn't supposed to start until six, so there were several of us who took advantage of the hour to use the facilities."

"Can you walk me through who did what when?" I asked.

"I was the first to leave the group and I went alone," Beth said. "I've been having some digestive issues lately and I excused myself to find the ladies' room shortly after we were shown to our table and Sam was taken to the locker room."

"And how long were you gone?" I asked.

"I guess about ten minutes."

"More like fifteen." Tammy Rhea snickered.

Beth gave Tammy a dirty look but didn't respond.

"Did anyone else leave the table?"

"Tammy Rhea and Emmy Jean excused themselves to freshen up shortly after I returned," Beth provided. "They were gone for at least as long as I was. In fact, they didn't get back until after Susan left to call her daughter."

"And what time was it when Susan left to call her daughter?"

"I guess around five-twenty the first time," Beth answered.

"The first time?"

"Susan first left when her daughter called," Janice explained. "She came back to the table about five minutes later. It was obvious she was agitated. She made a comment about needing to take care of something for her daughter and then left for a second time, although she said she'd try to make it back before Sam came back as Santa at six."

"But she never came back?"

"No, and I wasn't surprised. Susan and her daughter have a very odd relationship.

As we've said, whenever her daughter calls Susan drops everything and runs to her."

"And this would be her youngest daughter?" I knew Susan had four adult children.

"Yes. Her older three are settled into their own lives and I don't think Susan's divorce has affected them to the same degree it has her youngest."

"Did anyone else leave the group?"

Everyone agreed that no one else had left the table before my finding Sam dead in the alley.

"There are a lot of names on my list," I said. "Seven of these people are the ones who accompanied Sam to the party and four others—Steven, Walt, Ted, and Gil—followed Sam to the resort. Do any of you know what the twelve other people who were at the senior center when I called might have been doing?"

"Lucy Sanchez had a dinner party to attend," Janice offered.

"And Sonya James was going to her granddaughter's dance recital," Beth added.

No one else seemed to know what plans the others might have had.

"I guess we can call them," Elva suggested.

"That's a good idea," Beth agreed. "We'll do it tomorrow. I'll help you."

"And I'll call Ray Clark because I know him best," Janice offered. "Why don't the two of you," Janice looked at Luke and me, "see if you can pick up any leads at the places where Sam was known to spend time, the school and the soup kitchen?"

"Sounds like we have a plan," I agreed.

"You know, despite my reservations about getting the seniors involved with Sam's murder investigation I had a really nice day," I said to Luke after everyone had left. I was off again the next day and planned to stay over at Luke's another night.

"I was happy to spend some time with you, no matter what it was we were doing." Luke smiled.

"I was thinking about a tree." I turned my head so I was looking at Luke. "What do you think about going out tomorrow to get one for your great room?"

"I think I'd like that very much."

"There's a farm that sells really fresh Norfolk pines. Probably not the Christmas tree you're used to, but they can be really beautiful when decorated."

"We can make a day of it," Luke said. "We can buy the tree, go to the Christmas store for decorations, and then maybe grab some lunch. It'll be fun."

"Sounds perfect, but what about the senor potluck and our part of the investigation?"

"We'll get an early start and go to the school first thing."

"Not too early; it's my day to sleep in."

"Fine. We'll sleep as long as we want and then go to the school. After that we'll have breakfast and then get the tree. Once we know the size we end up with we can stop by the Christmas store for lights and ornaments. We'll bring everything here and then head over to the senior potluck. After that we should have at least a little bit of time to begin decorating the tree before we have to head over to the soup kitchen."

I yawned and leaned back in my chair. "Sounds good."

"I'm going to walk over to check on the horses before I begin locking up for the night. Do you want to come?"

Surprisingly, I did, considering that until I met a little darling named Lucifer I'd really, really hated horses. Not that they were my favorite animal even now. But having met Lucifer when he was only a day old and so very sweet and cute, and having visited as he'd grown into a monster of a horse, I could now say this one horse at least didn't terrify me at all.

Several other foals had been born to Luke's stable since we'd been dating. He hadn't kept them all, but I'd been able to spend enough time around horses that started off small and grew into huge that the mere thought of being trampled by one of the giant beasts didn't send me running the way it once had.

"How's my big boy?" I asked as Lucifer, a huge black stallion with a gentle disposition, trotted over to me the minute I entered the barn. He nuzzled my hand, looking for the treat he knew I always brought with me. Luke had a bin with apples and carrots we could pull from when we wanted to offer something to the horses.

The number of animals Luke maintained on the property changed depending on the season and his overall plan. Currently there were twelve horses on site that he had told me he'd probably maintain for the winter.

"Have you heard how Hoku is doing?" Hoku was the first foal I'd seen being born. Luke had let me name her and I'd chosen Hoku, which means star. About a month ago Luke had decided to sell her to one of his friends, and while I understood he was operating a business and business decisions needed to be made, it still made me sad that she was no longer part of the stable.

"She's very happy in her new home. We'll fly over to visit after the holidays."

Luke's friend lived on Maui, which was just a short flight from Oahu, and he had assured me I could visit any time I wanted.

I turned toward the door as Sandy and Luke's dogs, Duke and Dallas, wandered into the barn. When I'd first started bringing Sandy around he had barked at the horses, so he hadn't been allowed in the barn, but once he learned ranch etiquette he could roam freely when we visited.

"I missed this while you were gone," I said as Luke began topping off water barrels.

"I had a nice visit with my family, but I missed you and the animals more than I can say. I'm really glad to be home."

"Did your sister have her baby?"

"No, she has another month to go. My youngest sister is expecting as well, so it looks like by this time next year I'll be uncle to two bouncing bundles of joy."

"It's great that your sisters are having their children close together, especially if they turn out to be the same sex. Cousins can be important allies. Kekoa and I have been best friends all our lives, and there isn't a day that goes by that I'm not thankful for the fact that I have a cousin who's close in age."

"Sarah is having a girl, but it's too early to tell what the sex of Stephanie's baby will be. When I spoke to Stephanie she mentioned wanting a girl, but I think her husband would prefer a boy."

"I guess most men want sons, and I'm sure they're important to a ranching family. It's nice that your father has two sons interested in following in his footstep. I know it means a lot to my dad that all five of his sons followed in his."

Luke stopped what he was doing and looked at me. "Did your dad put any sort of pressure on your brothers to become cops?"

"No, not really. I guess he did raise them with the idea of becoming cops, but I can't remember any of my brothers fighting him on the idea. Did your dad put pressure on you to go into ranching?"

Luke frowned. "Not directly, but there's an underlying current between us that makes me aware that he wishes I'd move back to Texas, get married, buy some land, and start populating the earth with sons and cows."

"Do you ever consider doing that?" I tried not to show the fear I couldn't help but have.

"I love my life here and I much prefer horses to cows, but there are times when I feel like an outsider in my own family. It never bothered me before, but with both my sisters having kids I guess it's occurred to me that should I have children one day they wouldn't grow up with their uncles, aunts, and cousins the way my siblings' children will." Luke shook his head. "Not that children are even on the radar for me, but they most definitely are on my mom's."

"Neither of your brothers are married," I pointed out.

"Yes, but my youngest brother is in a fairly serious relationship. I won't be a bit surprised if an engagement isn't announced in the next few months."

"Did you have a chance to meet the girl when you were home?"

He nodded. "Her name is Willa. She's actually a friend of Courtney's, which I guess is how she met Matt in the first place."

"So you saw Courtney when you were home." Courtney Westlake was an old girlfriend of Luke's who had shown up on Oahu last summer on a whim, but she'd decided to return to Texas the previous September. I tried not to be a jealous girlfriend, but I had to admit I was over-the-moon happy when she left. Luke tried to tell me that she was just a friend, but as hard as I tried, I couldn't help but picture her in his arms on more than one occasion during the three weeks he was visiting his family.

"I did. She's doing well. She has a new job at a ranch that just happens to be next door to my oldest brother's."

I forced a smile. "That's good. I'm glad things worked out for her."

Luke was opening and closing the stalls one at a time as he checked each one of his valuable livestock. He had a pat and a treat for each horse, and they seemed thrilled for their chance in the spotlight as he made his way down the aisle.

"I'd love it if you'd consider coming home with me at some point. I know you've met my sisters briefly, but I want you to meet the whole family, and it would be great to show you around the place I grew up. I know it might be hard to get that much time off work, but if you could work it out I know we'd have fun."

The thought of going to Texas and meeting Luke's "people" both fascinated and terrified me. I was afraid I'd be as much out of my element as I initially thought Luke was here. Of course, he'd proved me wrong. He was so much more than a displaced cowboy once you got to know him. Still, based on what he'd just said, I had to believe he hadn't permanently left Texas behind.

"Maybe," I answered vaguely. "If I can get the time off."

"Just let me know when it might work for you and I'll make the arrangements. I think you'll love Texas. It's a lot different from Hawaii, but it has a charm that's all its own. And the people who live there are some of the friendliest you're ever likely to meet."

"I'll see what I can work out." I leaned my head against Lucifer's neck and took in his smell. Since when had I started liking horse smell? There was no doubt about it; my time with Luke was changing me. There was a part of me that feared that change and another that welcomed it more than I could say.

"That should do it," Luke declared as he entered the last stall. "Why don't you head back with the dogs and I'll turn everything off and meet you back at the house?"

"There's a beautiful sky tonight and the temperature has cooled considerably. It seems like it might be a nice night for a spa. If you aren't too tired, that is."

Luke smiled in return. My heart melted each time he gave me one of his smoldering looks that left little doubt in my mind that, whatever his long-term plans, in this moment he desired me as much as I desired him.

Chapter 6

Monday, December 19

It was the smell of coffee that pulled me out of the strange dream I was having. In it I was surfing while looking toward the shore, where Luke was sitting on a cow with a very pregnant Courtney sitting in front of him. I suppose the dream made sense in a twisted sort of way. I couldn't get the idea out of my mind that Courtney would make a much better wife for Luke than I ever would. She lived near his family and after seeing the way she looked at Luke when she'd been on the island the previous summer I was certain she'd be more than happy to have his babies and help him raise cows as his father hoped. I didn't have any experience being around cows, but I was pretty sure I wouldn't like them any more than I liked horses.

"Wake up, sleepyhead." Luke kissed me gently on the forehead. "I know you wanted to sleep in, but we need to get going if we're going to get everything on our list accomplished."

I groaned and rolled over.

He must have set the coffee I'd smelled on the bedside table because the next thing I knew Luke was using his hands and lips to nudge me awake in the most delightful way. I kissed him back as his lips moved from my neck to my mouth.

"Did I smell coffee?" I slowly opened my eyes.

"You did. I hoped it would wake you, but I have a better idea."

"Yeah?" I smiled.

"Yeah."

Ninety minutes later, Luke and I were heading toward the school where Sam had volunteered. The building was a single story, long and rectangular-shaped, with large windows that looked out onto the groomed grounds. After inquiring at the office we learned the reading program Sam had volunteered for was in a room at the end of the hall and the person in charge, Mahanna, was a woman about my age.

The petite Hawaiian waved at us as we entered. The large room was set up like a library, with bookshelves against every wall and tables arranged in groupings in the middle. "How can I help you?"

"I'm Lani and this is my friend, Luke. We hoped to speak to you about one of your volunteers, Sam Riverton."

Mahanna lowered her eyes. "I heard what happened. I am so very sorry. Sam was a good man."

"It's been a shock to us all."

"I'll have one of the volunteers cover for me so we can find a more private place to talk." Mahanna gestured to one of the older women who was reading with some kids. She said a few words to her and then led us through the door and back into the hall. "There shouldn't be anyone in the cafeteria at this time of day. We can talk in there."

The cafeteria looked exactly like the one in the school I'd attended while growing up. Dark brown tables with bench seating were lined up in rows against the walls. There were silver doors covering the windows that separated the dining area from the kitchen and blue trays were stacked and waiting for the first of the grade-school kids to come in for their midday meal. I didn't know what was on the menu that day, but something smelled wonderful.

"What would you like to know?" Mahanna asked.

"Luke and I were friends of Sam's. We've been speaking to his friends, neighbors, and associates, trying to make sense of what happened. We were hoping you could tell us about Sam and his work here."

"Sam was great. He'd been volunteering for the past two years. He came in two or three afternoons a week, doing whatever needed to be done. The kids loved him."

"How about the staff and the other volunteers?"

"Everyone loved Sam. He was a genuinely happy person who shared his sunny disposition. I was shocked when I read in the newspaper that he'd been murdered. As far as I know, he didn't have any enemies."

"Did you know Sam well?" I asked.

"No, not really," Mahanna admitted. "He didn't really share all that much about his life outside of his volunteer work with us. He did say he was a widower and that he'd found relief from his grief by helping others. I don't know that I can tell you anything that might help you to find his killer, but I'm sure he didn't deserve to die."

"Do you know if Sam had relationships—friendships—with any of the staff or volunteers outside the school?"

Mahanna paused. "There's one volunteer you might want to speak to. Her name is Riva Spencer. I know they occasionally went to lunch before their shift."

Riva's name was on Steven's list. While there was a regular group of seniors who played bingo regularly who I knew well, there were others who popped in and out, and I didn't know them other than in passing. Riva was one of the ones who played sporadically. "Is Riva here today?"

"No. But I can call her, and if she's willing to speak to you I can give you her number."

"That would be very helpful."

"The bell is about to ring for recess. I'll make the call once the kids go out into the yard. You can wait or I can call or text you after I've spoken to Riva."

"I'll give you my number and you can text us. The delicious smell coming from the kitchen has made me hungry. I think we'll go grab something."

Luke and I decided to get a quick bite at the food truck on the beach. We were both hungry, but it was too late to eat a big meal with the potluck just a few hours away. Besides, it was a beautiful, sunny day with temperatures in the midseventies; sitting on a picnic bench overlooking the sea dotted with surfers and sharing a sandwich seemed to be the perfect choice.

"Boy, am I glad to see the two of you," Komo Kamaka, the owner of the food truck, greeted us. "Been a while since you've been by."

"I've been working a lot of extra shifts and Luke was on the mainland," I told him.

"Then I guess you might not know about the new truck that's been working the area."

"I hadn't heard," I admitted. "Is there a problem with it?"

"It's run by some haole who doesn't understand our ways. Those of us who have been working the beach have been doing so for years and have learned to operate in a cooperative manner, but this new guy is a real piece of work. Most of us think he's planning to monopolize the food truck business and push everyone else out. Some of the other food vendors are pretty upset, and there's talk of using force to shut him down. I want the man gone as bad as the next guy, but I'm a peaceful man. I'd rather find a nonviolent way to return order to the beach."

"Have you tried talking to him?" Luke asked.

"I have. He seemed disinclined to listen to my advice. I'm afraid that if things do get violent it might have a negative effect on all of us. I was hoping maybe Luke could have a talk with him."

"Why me?" Luke asked.

"He's a white boy like you. I hoped he might listen to you."

"I'm not sure that's true, but I'd be happy to talk to him if you think it might help. Where can I find him?'

"Just follow the huge banners he's set up all up and down the beach, directing people to buy a burger for a buck. A buck? I've heard rumors he doesn't even use real beef."

"Okay. I'll see what I can do."

We took our sandwiches to one of the picnic tables overlooking the water. It was such a beautiful day that I found myself wishing I had time for an actual day off. It seemed as if life had been so busy lately that I barely had time to do the things that made life worthwhile.

"It's been weeks since I had time to surf. The waves are calling," I said.

"It does seem like a perfect day to spend on the water. I haven't found the time to head to the beach since I've been back."

"Maybe we can go surfing on Thursday if Sam's murder is wrapped up and I end up with my normal day off."

"Have you heard from Jason today?"

I wadded up the wrappers from our food and tossed them into the green trash can that was chained to the table. "No. I guess I should call him. He seems to have accepted my snooping around as long as I stay in contact, share my information, and leave all the dangerous work to him."

"That sounds like a good arrangement."

"It is. I think Jason would rather I stay out of it altogether, but he doesn't want the senior brigade going off on their own so he's tolerating my involvement." I looked down at my phone, which had just buzzed. It was a text from Mahanna.

"What does she say?" Luke asked.

"Riva Spencer is happy to speak to us, but she's off the island today and wants me to call her tomorrow." I looked out to the sea. "I know it's important to follow up on even the smallest clue in these types of situations, but I feel like we're on the wrong track."

"Even if we are, I don't suppose it can hurt to speak to the people Sam knew best."

I sighed. "Yeah. You're right. But tomorrow is soon enough to continue our quest. Right now I say we take a break to buy that Christmas tree we've been talking about."

"I could use some holiday cheer."

The tree lot wasn't busy at this time of day, so Luke and I were able to stroll through the rows of trees, chatting quietly while Christmas music played in the background. The fir trees cut on the mainland and shipped over were already half dead, but the pines grown on the island and only recently cut were lush and green.

"You have a high ceiling in your living area, so I say you get a tall tree. At least twelve feet."

"We'll need a lot of lights to cover a twelve-foot tree."

"Yes, but think how pretty it will be. If you don't want to buy a lot of ornaments we can string popcorn or make a paper chain, like I used to when I was a kid."

"It seems so odd to be buying a Christmas tree when it's so hot," Luke commented.

"What would the temperature be like back home?"

"It can vary from year to year, but most of the time it's in the midforties in December. As I said, we get snow from time to time, but it definitely isn't a given. Still, there's usually a chill in the air by the time Christmas rolls around."

"Does your family always do it up big?"

"Always. My mother and sisters start baking the week before Thanksgiving and don't stop until December 26, when everyone goes on a diet. It's the custom in our family for everyone to go Christmas tree shopping together the first weekend in December."

"So you must have gone with your family when you were home."

"I did and it was fun." Luke turned and pulled me into his arms. He gently kissed me on the lips before taking a step back. "But this is a lot more fun. I'm glad we're able to do this for our first Christmas together. I feel like maybe we're starting a new tradition."

I wound my right arm through Luke's left as we continued to walk through the rows of trees. I'd never stopped to wonder what it would be like to prepare for Christmas in a climate where heavy sweaters at the least were the norm and the possibility of snow actually existed.

"Other than baking and tree shopping, what else does your family do?"

"The town we live in is made up of close-knit ranching families. Ever since the town was founded they've all shown up on the weekend after Thanksgiving to help decorate. Wreaths are hung on the lampposts that border both sides of the main thoroughfare through town and white lights are hung in all the trees. The local merchants decorate their windows, and on the first Friday in December everyone comes out for the annual tree lighting. It's a special time. But enough about my Christmas. Tell me what I can expect from yours."

I picked a Santa hat off the rack near the cash register and plopped it on my head. "Like your family, mine has always had a tree, although we had a fake one. We exchange gifts on Christmas Day after eating a huge brunch hosted by either Mom or one of the aunts. My siblings, cousins, and I usually go surfing while someone roasts a pig for Christmas dinner. The entire Pope family gathers to share the meal. Most years we eat outdoors off paper plates, but it's always special."

"It sounds really nice. Do you do something special on Christmas Eve?"

"Most of the time Christmas Eve is reserved for the immediate family, but Jason has already announced that he's going to his in-laws this year and a couple of my other brothers have to work. I don't think Mom is planning to do anything much this year."

"Why don't we have a party?" Luke suggested. "We can have it at my house because there's more room there than there is in your condo. We can invite the condo family, as well as any of the seniors who don't have anywhere to go."

I stopped walking and turned to look at Luke. "That would be really fun. I know Kekoa's family isn't doing anything much this year, and Cam is always at loose ends. I'll ask Elva and the others from the complex. It'll be awesome." I looked up at the tall tree I was standing next to. "We have a lot to do in the next few days, beginning with buying a tree. What do you think of this one?"

"It's perfect. If we hurry we'll have time to stop off to buy some decorations before the potluck."

The seniors had gone all out for the potluck. Not only did a total of twenty-three people bring food but they all brought enough food to feed everyone. In other words, there was a lot of food. I didn't necessarily think a potluck was the best time to discuss a murder case, but the seniors had news and seemed determined to share it.

"Beth and I have narrowed down the list to those members of the center who were present when you called Sam and don't have an alibi," Elva began. "You've already mentioned Walt, Ted, and Gil were at the resort with Steven when Sam was killed. Steven also told you they saw you show Sam to the locker room, and it seems to us any one of them could have followed Sam into the alley."

"I've already given my brother Jason that information and he's agreed to speak to each of the four men individually," I explained.

"We've tried to get in touch with Susan, but she isn't answering her cell," Beth added. "Stella Gold was with her family at a dinner party at her sister's home, which the sister has confirmed. The only person who was at the center at the time of the call that doesn't seem to have an alibi is Cliff Wells," Elva finished.

Cliff had a temper and the physical ability to hit someone over the head hard enough to kill him.

"What did he say when you asked about his alibi?" I wondered.

"That it was none of our damn business what he did after he left the senior center."

That sounded like something Cliff would say. I doubted he was guilty, but it wouldn't hurt to follow up with him.

"Has anyone heard from Janice?" I asked. "When I spoke to her last night she said she would be here today."

"I left a message for her shortly after we arrived but I haven't heard back," Beth shared. "I hope she's okay. She seems to be taking Sam's death really hard. We all are, but Janice more than everyone else."

"Maybe Luke and I should stop by her place after we leave here. I'm kind of worried about her."

"She was going to speak to RJ Clark," Tammy Rhea reminded us. "Maybe she just got held up."

"You'd think she would have called," Beth countered. "She must know we'll worry if she doesn't show up."

"Maybe she lay down for a nap and didn't wake up in time. Lord knows I've done that a time or two," Elva supplied.

"Yeah, maybe." I glanced at Luke. He had a worried look on his face too.

Luke changed the somber mood by bringing up the Christmas Eve party he'd suggested to me. The senior gang immediately took off their sleuthing hats and replaced them with their party planning ones. Everyone was even more enthusiastic than I'd thought they would be about Luke's offer to celebrate Christmas Eve at the ranch.

"I wonder if we should do another potluck?" Emmy Jean asked. "Word got out at the senior center about this one, so I think you should plan on having a fairly large crowd. It'll be easier if you provide the pig and ask everyone else to bring something to share."

"The pig?" Luke asked.

"To roast," Elva said.

Luke glanced at me and I nodded. A pig was traditional.

"We don't have a lot of time to prepare things," Emmy Jean stated. "The girls and I will start calling around and asking everyone to bring a dish to share. Other than the senior crowd, who else are you inviting?"

"The people from the condos where I live," I provided. "There are ten of us there, including me and Elva. And a few people from the resort," I added. "Maybe five or ten."

"Okay, then. We just need someone to dig the pit," Emmy Jean declared.

Once the ladies got to organizing they were very efficient. Elva knew someone they could hire to not only prepare the hole for roasting but to prepare the pig as well. Given the short time we had to get everything ready, Luke agreed the expense of paying someone would be well worth it.

Emmy Jean started a shopping list and before I knew it, five women were planning a trip into town to buy the items we'd need with a fist full of cash Luke had given them.

"I'm sorry this party has gotten totally out of hand," I said to Luke after we managed to slip out of the potluck.

Luke shrugged. "It's okay. I can see that planning the party is making the gals happy, and it will be nice to provide a place for everyone to gather and share a meal."

"It did seem like there was a new energy among the ladies, but are you sure it's okay that someone's going to dig a pit in your pasture? It doesn't seem like a huge pit is very horse friendly."

"I'm not using that pasture for the horses at the moment and I probably won't in the near future unless I expand quite a bit. I can always fill in the pit if I need to. I do think I might need some additional tables and chairs, though."

"There's a place I know where you can rent them. Renting at this late date would be easier, but I could probably borrow some. I'll ask the condo family tonight when I get home, though if I know Elva, she'll beat me to it."

"You know I want this to be our party and I definitely want your input, but I also know you have a busy week coming up at work. Leave the grunt work to me."

I smiled as I wound my fingers through Luke's as he drove toward Janice's house. Suddenly the upcoming holiday had a shiny, new feel to it, and I found I was more excited about Christmas than I'd been in a long time.

"Janice's car is in the drive," I said.

"Maybe she really did just fall asleep."

"I'll go knock on the door. Why don't you wait here? I don't want to embarrass her if she was napping."

I knocked, but there wasn't a response. Then I rang the doorbell several times just to be certain. It was possible she'd gone somewhere with someone else, which would explain the car in the driveway, but I hated to just leave in case she was hurt or worse. She was at the age where something like a stroke or heart attack could come out of nowhere. Life must be hard once you reached the three-quarter-century mark.

I turned and looked back toward the truck where Luke was waiting. I shrugged and decided to ring the bell one more time. No one answered. I was about to leave when someone peeked through the peephole in the door. When Janice opened the door I saw she was wearing an old robe and her hair was mussed. It appeared she had been napping.

"Lani, what are you doing here?"

"We missed you at the potluck," I explained. "I know you planned to be there, so I wanted to check to make sure you were okay."

"I'm fine, dear. Thanks for stopping by."

Janice began to close the door without asking me in.

"Who is it?" RJ Clark was standing behind Janice.

I couldn't help but blush. Apparently, Janice hadn't been napping after all.

"I'm sorry to bother you," I choked out as I tried to cover my embarrassment. "I was worried when Janice didn't show up at the potluck. I didn't realize she had company."

Janice giggled when RJ leaned over and whispered something in her ear.

I knew I should probably just leave, but for some reason I just stood there and stared at the scantily clad couple.

"I asked RJ to stop by so we could discuss the situation with Sam and I'm afraid we got distracted and lost track of time," Janice explained. "But no need to worry. I can assure you that I'm fine."

"I guess so. Everyone was worried."

"Do apologize for me. Now, I have to go. I'll call you tomorrow."

With that, Janice closed the door in my face.

I wanted to be offended, but I just laughed instead. Maybe life at the three-quarter-century mark wasn't as bad as I'd imagined.

Chapter 7

The soup kitchen where Sam had volunteered was staffed with men and women from the community who served food donated by businesses as well as individuals. Many of the people who came there for a meal lived in a tent city down by the beach, while others resided in shelters around town. Everyone seemed to know one another, so the environment in the cheerily decorated room was much like that of a large, boisterous family sharing an evening meal.

We didn't see Walt Goodman when we first arrived, so Luke and I decided to split up and talk to whoever was willing to speak to us. Joshua Simon had been accurate when he'd told us Sam was a popular guy. Once Luke made it clear to everyone why we were there, almost everyone stopped eating to share memories of him. Because Luke seemed to have the people eating meals covered, I made my way into the kitchen to help with the dishes and chat with the volunteers who wandered in and out of the heart of the kitchen.

"I really appreciate your helping out," a petite woman with a long gray braid thanked me when she entered the room with a large, almost empty bowl that looked as if it had contained mashed potatoes.

"I'm happy to help. It's a good thing you're doing here."

"I can't take credit. It's really Joshua's program."

"It may be his program, but it takes more than the effort of one man to make something like this work. My name is Lani, by the way."

"I'm Tina."

I realized this woman could well be the woman Sam had supposedly stolen from Walt. Of course, Tina wasn't an unusual name, but it wasn't supercommon either.

"Your friend mentioned you're here to ask about Sam," Tina added.

I nodded.

"It's such a shame what happened to him. He was a good man."

"That seems to be the general opinion of him. Did you know him well?"

She shrugged, but I could see she was fighting tears. "Well enough to know he didn't deserve to die the way he did. Don't get me wrong; Sam could have a cranky side, but he'd give you the shirt off his back if you needed it."

"So there wasn't anyone who didn't like Sam?"

She didn't answer.

"I didn't know him well," I added, "but he attended functions at the senior center where I sometimes hang out and I agree he was a good man. I can only think of a handful of people who would disagree with that assessment."

"Really? Who?"

"His brother for one," I fished. "It seems they mended fences, but I have reason to believe they were on the outs for a while."

"Well, sure. Disagreements within families are common."

"I also heard he had a way with the ladies that led to a few problems."

"Sam was a charmer and attracted his share of female attention, but he would never approach a woman who belonged to someone else, despite what some people might say."

I turned the water on and began rinsing one of the pans. "I had the same impression of him, but one of his friends—a man named Walter—seemed to be furious with Sam for stealing his girlfriend."

"I wasn't his girlfriend."

"You were the woman Sam stole from Walter?" I tried to look innocent, but based on the suspicion on Tina's face I wasn't sure I'd pulled it off.

"If you and your friend are here to find out whether Walt killed Sam over some silly rivalry, you're barking up the wrong tree. Sure, Walt showed interest in the two of us developing a relationship, but I never did or said anything to indicate to him that I was interested in the same thing. Besides, Sam and I were just friends. Not that I wouldn't have wanted more, but that wasn't what he was interested in. I'm pretty sure he had his sights on someone else."

"Do you know who?"

"No. I'm sorry, I don't."

After spending two hours chatting with people at the soup kitchen Luke and I realized there wasn't anything more to learn and headed back to his place to trim the tree. Although we'd both eaten a lot of food at the potluck, we were both a bit hungry, so he made us sandwiches while I called Jason, who said he had pretty much eliminated everyone on his suspect list for one reason or another. Walt Goodman never had shown up at the soup kitchen, but Jason had spoken to him and he felt Walt's style of retribution for stealing his girl fell more along the lines of embarrassing Sam rather than murdering him. Besides, Jason told me, Walt didn't seem physically able to bash someone's head in.

"Did you recover Sam's phone with his other things?" I asked.

"No, though I did pull his phone records. The last person he spoke to was you at about two o'clock."

"That was when I called him to ask if he'd be willing to play Santa at the party. The man we hired called in sick."

"Of all the people you know, why did you call Sam?" Jason asked.

"I knew he had a Santa suit. I first met Sam a little over a year ago at a party the senior center threw. Elva asked me to go with her. Sam was new to the group, but for some reason he had a suit and agreed to hand out the gifts everyone brought for the exchange. He did a wonderful job and seemed to enjoy it, so when Kekoa told me that she was short one Santa I thought of him."

"How long was it between the time you called Sam and the time he arrived at the resort?"

"About three hours. He was due to start at six and arrived at around five. Did you speak to his ex?"

"Yes, and she has an alibi of sorts."

"What do you mean by that?"

"She claims to have been at home, but she provided a neighbor who saw her go outside to get her mail. It's a weak alibi and it's possible the neighbor is just covering for her, but for now I don't have any reason to hold her, so there isn't a lot I can do unless new information comes to light."

"How did she seem when you spoke to her?" I wondered.

"She was upset. I asked about the lawsuit she was supposedly threatening Sam with and she said she wasn't planning to follow through with it."

"That's what Steven said as well, although the whole thing seems pretty odd."

"She really doesn't seem to have a motive. She basically lived off the alimony Sam sent her every month, which seems like a pretty good reason for her to want him alive."

"Yeah, I agree. I don't think she's a strong suspect."

"I also spoke to most of the other people on the list you gave me. I've been able to clear all but two of the people you believed knew Sam was at the resort."

"Who are they?"

"Susan Oberman hasn't answered the phone or returned any of my messages, and when I tried to speak to Cliff Wells, he told me to either arrest him or leave him alone."

"Sounds like Cliff. And Susan is bad about returning calls." I took a deep breath and slowly let it out. "I really doubt Susan killed Sam. Unless there's something I don't know, she had no reason to. And as prickly as Cliff is, I don't see him as the killer either. Because you seem to have eliminated pretty much everyone, I think I'm going to refocus."

"What do you mean?" Jason asked.

"I'm thinking Sam wasn't the target, at least not specifically. I can't decide whether the man who was originally supposed to play Santa was the target and the killer didn't know about the switch and killed the wrong man, or if there was something going on in the alley Sam just happened to stumble onto."

"I've considered both of those scenarios," Jason said. "I've checked out the man who was supposed to play Santa and haven't come up with a reason for anyone to want him dead, and I spoke to his wife, who confirmed he *was* home sick with the flu. It was dark in the alley and whatever happened was quick. Given the fact that there were no defensive wounds on Sam's body I'm guessing either there was someone waiting for Sam to arrive or he stumbled on to something he wasn't meant to see and ended up dead because he was in the wrong place at the wrong time. I know you've been really busy with all those extra shifts, but can you think of anything odd that's been going on at Dolphin Bay recently?"

"Well, there's been a larger than usual turnover in personnel lately. There's a new general manager who seems to be rubbing everyone the wrong way, so a lot of people are looking for other jobs. Coupled with the flu epidemic, which has everyone who isn't sick working jobs they aren't trained for, emotions are high. I heard a waiter in the steak house almost stabbed one of the chefs in the main kitchen with a carving knife when he criticized the way he did his job."

"I suppose added tension could lead to violence. Anything else?"

"There's been something strange going on with the paychecks. A couple of employees noticed a weird deduction they'd never seen before. It was only a dollar or two, but if you multiply that by all the employees at the resort over time, it could add up to a chunk of money. I heard the head bookkeeper is being investigated for embezzlement, although she's denying it. She claims the deduction was nothing more than a computer error that wasn't caught right away. And then, of course, there are the burglaries."

"I know HPD was called in when a few high-dollar items were reported stolen. Have there been other incidents?"

"Yeah, but management took care of the claims for the items reported missing with a negligible dollar value rather than calling in the police, which would send the wrong message to the guests."

"You mean the message that you have a thief in your midst and they should consider another lodging option if they're traveling with any items of value?"

"Yep, that's it exactly."

I hung up with Jason and joined Luke, who was already hanging lights on the tree. I filled him in on my conversation while we worked side by side to bring some Christmas cheer to Luke's living space. I was juggling so many emotions I wasn't sure which one to focus on. I was excited for us to spend our first Christmas together, I was anxious about getting everything ready for the party now that we'd committed to it, frustrated with the investigation into Sam's death because we didn't seem to be getting anywhere with it, and worried about how the seniors would take it if it ended up one of those cases that never were solved. Add to that my unhappiness at the idea that I needed to return to work the next day. I usually liked my job and didn't mind going in, but tonight I was a bundle of nerves, ready to explode should the least little thing go wrong.

"What do you think?" Luke asked as he plugged in the last strand of lights and flipped the switch.

"It's beautiful. I can't wait to see how it looks with the other decorations we bought."

"I have a feeling I'll have to buy more, but we can hang what we have. Hand me that red bag."

It felt homey and romantic, decorating a tree with Luke. I thought of it as *our* tree, which added to my nervousness following Luke's revelation that his family was still hoping he'd move back to Texas.

"When we were at the soup kitchen today one of the volunteers told me they needed more people to help deliver Santa baskets. It's just a few hours on Wednesday and Thursday nights. I thought I'd volunteer. Want to do it with me?" Luke asked.

"I have to work on Wednesday, but I'd like to help out on Thursday."

"Okay, great. I'll sign us both up. I know we were at the soup kitchen to get the dirt on Sam, but I enjoyed contributing to a good cause. I think I might sign up to do it one day a week after the holidays."

"If you want to do it on Thursdays I'll join you, provided Drake doesn't mess with my schedule again."

Of all the WSOs I worked with, Drake Longboard was the only one I absolutely couldn't stand. In addition to the fact that he was a jerk, he'd been promoted to the position of assistant to the head WSO despite the fact that both Cam and I had more experience, more saves, and had been at the resort longer. Drake wasn't any fonder of me than I was of him and seemed to take great joy in messing with my schedule simply because he could.

"Maybe we should relax with a glass of wine before I take you home," Luke suggested. "I can finish this tomorrow. You look beat."

"I guess I am tired. I have a feeling this is going to be a very long week. I just hope everyone being out sick doesn't mess with my having the entire weekend off. I put in for Christmas Eve a year ago and Christmas is on Sunday, my regular day off."

"I'll have everyone come over after your shift on Saturday just in case you do get called in," Luke said. "I was thinking of hiring a car to provide rides so people don't have to drive home after they've been drinking."

"That's a good idea, especially for the seniors. Not that they're big drinkers, but a lot of them have trouble driving after dark."

"I thought I'd call the private limo company my mom used when she was here with my sisters last summer. It's kind of short notice, but my mom tends to tip big, so maybe they'll find a way to accommodate us. I'm assuming you'll just stay over?"

I hadn't thought about it. It would be nice to wake up with Luke on Christmas morning. I'd already invited him to dinner at my parents' on Christmas Day. Spending the entire holiday together would be nice.

Suddenly I remembered I hadn't bought Luke a gift. I normally did my Christmas shopping during the off season, when I had time to make a trip to the south shore, but Luke and I hadn't been a couple at the time I'd made the trip, so I hadn't thought to get him anything.

"What's wrong?" Luke asked. "You have a look of panic on your face. Don't you want to stay over?"

"I do. Of course I do. It's just that I remembered something I need to do but forgot about. I'll need to be sure to get to it tomorrow. Now, how about that glass of wine you promised me?"

Chapter 8

Wednesday, December 21

I'd ended up working a double shift on Tuesday, so I hadn't seen Luke since he dropped me off at my condo on Monday night. I knew he was delivering gifts this evening, but he didn't think he'd be late and had promised to stop by my place after he was finished. So far no one had asked me to stay after my shift, which had ended at five, and so far I still had all day Thursday off as well.

It was a warm, sunny day without a cloud in the sky. Normally I don't give a second thought to celebrating Christmas in the heat and humidity, but as Luke and I had relaxed with our wine on Monday evening, he'd told me some stories from Christmases in his past, many of which included snow, and the idea of a white Christmas had seeded and taken root. Not this year for sure, but maybe next year?

I found myself daydreaming of romantic sleigh rides as Luke and I cuddled under a warm blanket. And it would be fun to have a real wood fire to ward off the chill as snow fell gently outside the window. The town where Luke had grown up sounded charming and I could almost smell the scent of the pine boughs they used around town as decoration.

There was a time when I wouldn't have considered being away from my family for the holiday, but it seemed we were becoming more and more fragmented as my brothers married and developed Christmas traditions of their own. Jason had to juggle time with our family and his wife's, and my mom still wasn't getting along with my youngest brother, Jeff's new wife, which had led to their decision to fly to the mainland this year to spend Christmas with her family.

Kekoa's family dynamic was all off as well because her parents had separated and her sister had gone to college on the mainland. Each year that went by seemed to result in a smaller and smaller group. Maybe it was time to establish new ways of doing things.

I glanced out over the water. I was working the family beach today. I much preferred the excitement of the surfing beach, but at least here, where pail-toting toddlers littered the beach, was better than the family pool. The tide coming into the north shore had created waves of a decent size, though this beach was protected by a reef, making for a calm body of water for kids of all ages.

Generally, the family beach was an easy gig. Most rescues involved bandaging skinned knees and recommending a cure for sunburn rather than actually heading out into the water to find a swimmer who had submerged and not reappeared.

"Excuse me, miss."

I looked down at a sunburned woman in a wide-brimmed hat and a yellow one-piece swimsuit who was standing at the foot of my tower.

"How can I help you?"

"I'm looking for my son Tommy. He asked me if he could walk down the beach to look for new shells to add to his collection, but that was thirty minutes ago. He should have returned by now."

I jumped down from the tower and landed with both feet in the sand. "Can you describe your son?"

"He's ten, about four feet ten inches tall. He has dark brown hair. Curly. And he has brown eyes."

"What is he wearing?"

"Blue swim trunks with a white stripe. He doesn't have a T-shirt on and his feet are bare. It's really not like him to simply wander away. He's very responsible for his age."

"Was he with anyone?"

"No, he was alone. He's an only child and we're here on vacation, so he doesn't know anyone."

Looking for lost kids was a common chore on the family beach, so at this point I wasn't all that concerned that he was missing. "I'll take a look to see if I can find him. I'm going to call for backup first, though, so the tower is covered. Do you have a cell phone?"

She held up her phone.

I handed the woman a card. "Call this number if you find him. If I or another WSO locates him first someone from headquarters will call you."

I couldn't help but notice the fear in the woman's eyes.

"Try not to worry. The beach is crowded today. It's hard to pick out an individual. He's probably in the vicinity. We'll find him."

I called Cam, who was covering the switchboard. He got someone to cover for him and came to help me look for the missing child. If I ever had kids and took them to a crowded place where they might get lost I wouldn't dress them in blue shorts. There were hundreds of kids in blue shorts. No, my little darling would be wearing fluorescent green or bright orange, a color that would stand out in a crowd.

"Makena is on her way over too," Cam informed me once he reached the tower.

I filled Cam in on the kid's name and description. "I'll head to the jetty; you head down the sand toward the surfing beach as soon as Makena gets here. He may have wandered over there when he noticed the awesome waves. Have Makena cover the tower." I took off at a jog with my rescue can hooked over my shoulder.

I really loved being a lifeguard, but any time a kid was missing for any length of time, or at risk of drowning after being tumbled off a raft or buried by a wave, it caused my heart to race and my adrenaline to increase significantly. While I've never lost a child in my care, I know there are fatalities every year on the beaches of the world that span the entire age spectrum. The water is an awesome place to be on a hot, humid day, but it can be a dangerous place to be as well. Visitors who came to the ocean for the first time often didn't understand the power of a riptide or the weight of a wave as it crashed over you. I took my job seriously and I'd been able to head off any number of tragedies before they'd developed, but with each minute that went by with no sign of Tommy, my heart raced just a little bit faster.

"Lani to tower one," I said into my handheld radio.

"Go for tower one," Makena answered.

"Any sign of Tommy?"

"No, I'm afraid not. There are a million kids out here today, but I haven't seen anyone fitting the description his mother gave."

I put my hand to my forehead to shade my eyes and looked out toward the water. There were dozens of heads bobbing up and down with the movement of the waves.

"Take a look at the jetty with the binoculars," I instructed Makena. "Do you see anyone at the end on one of the rocks near the waterline? I thought I noticed a movement."

I waited for a minute while Makena confirmed what I thought I'd seen. "Ten four. There's a kid climbing on the rocks near the waterline. The tide's coming in. He's going to get buried if he doesn't get out of there."

"I'm going after him. Let Cam know what I'm doing."

The waves crashing onto the rock structure created a noise too loud for me to be heard, so yelling at the kid to come in wouldn't do any good. I tried waving my arms as well as my rescue can as I made my way along the rocks. There were signs everywhere warning people to stay off the rocks, but the boy, who I was pretty sure was Tommy, wasn't the first to ignore the signs.

I was halfway along the jetty when a large wave came in and covered Tommy. When the wave receded he was no longer on the rock. I searched the water frantically but didn't see him.

"Tower one, it's Lani. Tommy is in the water. I repeat, in the water. I don't see him. I'm going in. Send backup."

I set my radio down and dove off the rock.

The thing about the current near the jetty was that it tended to circle back onto itself, creating a situation where a single strong wave can cause you to be thrown onto the rocks and pulled under by the current. It's a very unsafe area in which to swim, even for an experienced lifeguard. I used all my strength to clear the current before diving down to see if I could find Tommy before it was too late.

The water near the jetty was so choppy that it churned up the sand, making visibility almost nil. I surfaced at the point where I'd seen Tommy go in, but there still was no sign of him. I looked back toward the beach where other WSOs were running to help me. I just hoped our effort would be a rescue operation and not a retrieval.

I got my bearings and dove back down, trying to predict where Tommy might have drifted. The current seemed to be working its way around the front of the jetty, so I focused my mind and began swimming in that direction. The entire time I swam I imagined having to tell Tommy's mother that I'd gotten to him too late, that her son was never coming home. Just the thought of such a heart-wrenching conversation made me swim even harder and hold my breath a bit longer. When I got to the point where I couldn't hold my breath another second I surfaced and tread water while I looked around, trying to get my bearings. I could see Cam on the jetty, pointing to something in the distance. I turned and saw a flash of blue. I took a deep breath, then swam as fast as I could in that direction.

By the time I reached Tommy he wasn't breathing. I secured his body with my rescue can and began mouth-to-mouth resuscitation. The whole time I worked on him I prayed I hadn't been too late. Cam reached me after several minutes and together we swam him to the shore while continuing mouth-to-mouth the best we could in the choppy water. Cam had Tommy up on the beach just as an ambulance pulled onto the sand. Tears streamed down my face, first out of fear and then out of relief, as Tommy choked up a lungful of water and took his first breath.

Random people from the beach began hugging and congratulating me. I took a deep breath and willed my heart to slow as Tommy's mother joined him and the ambulance took off to the hospital.

"That was a close one," Cam said after he'd managed to separate me from the crowd.

"Tell me about it. Another minute and we might have lost him. I'm so glad you saw him."

"I was lucky. A flash of color caught my eye."

I stopped walking and looked back at the jetty. "The signs aren't enough. I know management feels a fence would take away from the aesthetics of the place, but one of these days someone's going to die."

Cam put his arm around me and walked me back to headquarters, where I took a short break before finishing my shift.

I was sitting in the resort lobby, chatting with Kekoa and checking my emails, when my phone buzzed, letting me know I had a new message.

"What's wrong?" I asked when I called Elva back. She'd never called me at work before, so I had to assume it was an emergency.

"Nothing's wrong, dear. It's just that the girls and I were chatting and we think it could be beneficial to reenact Sam's murder."

"Reenact it?"

"It was Tammy Rhea's idea, and it's a good one. One of us can pretend to be the body while the others act out different scenarios. Then we can try to whittle things down to the one that makes the most sense."

"That's a really good plan," I admitted.

"Do you remember how the alley looked that night? Where Sam fell, where the dumpsters and other things were located, the direction Sam was facing when he fell?"

"Yeah, I think I remember everything fairly accurately. We'll need to meet after four. The loading dock is crawling with people right now."

"Four works for us if it works for you."

"Make it four-thirty. I don't get off until five, but I think I can get Cam to cover for me for the last half hour of my shift. I'll meet you at the registration desk."

By the time the seniors and I headed out to the alley it was completely deserted. I'd borrowed a blanket from housekeeping so whoever played Sam could lay down on it after he was killed if necessary. I explained where he would have been coming from and where he most likely would have been attacked, given the position in which his body was found. I could tell that while the women were determined to find Sam's killer, being in the alley where he died was stirring emotions that were difficult to suppress.

"It feels so odd to stand in the place where Sam took his last breath," Elva whispered.

"I keep looking over my shoulder, expecting to see his ghost," Tammy Rhea agreed softly.

"Surely you don't believe in ghosts?" Beth challenged her.

"Of course I do. I've seen many in my lifetime."

Beth just rolled her eyes.

"We should retrace Sam's steps," I suggested before a fight broke out.

"The most direct route from the locker room to the back door of this building is along this line," Janice indicated, walking in a straight line toward the back door.

"But you said Sam's body was found over here." Emmy Jean stood in the location where I remembered finding it being.

"He must have seen something that made him veer off course," Tammy Rhea suggested.

They had a point. The placement of Sam's body made no sense if he'd simply been walking from the locker room to the party via the most direct route. "I wonder what he saw," I mused.

"Or who," Elva added.

"There were two gaps in the security tape. One at five twenty-nine and another at five fifty-three. My guess is that someone went through the door at five twenty-nine and then reentered the building at five fifty-three. The camera wouldn't have caught the actual murder because it only focused on the doorway and the loading dock itself, but it would have shown the identity of the person who came out to the alley, which, logic dictates, would be the killer."

"Didn't you say Sam was hit from behind?" Beth asked.

"Yes. That was how it looked."

"And yet it appeared he was walking toward someone or something."

"There most likely had to have been two people involved," I realized. "Whoever Sam was walking toward and whoever hit him from behind."

"Unless someone saw what happened I don't see how we're ever going to figure this out," Elva complained. "If the killer had turned out to be someone with a grudge against Sam, we might be able to figure that out, but if it's some random person or persons who was doing something and didn't want to be interrupted, I don't know how we'll ever figure out who it was."

Elva was right. This might be one mystery we couldn't solve.

"Let's take the time to go through this step by step," Emmy Jean said. "Beth, you pretend to be Sam. Go down the alley a bit and then walk in this direction toward the doorway. When I tell you to stop, turn and look toward me. I'll stand where whoever or whatever Sam must have seen would most likely have been. When you get to the blanket where Lani says the body was found, Tammy Rhea will pretend to hit you with something. Then fall forward and lay on your stomach."

Everyone got into place and Beth and Tammy Rhea did as Emmy Jean had instructed.

"Here's the problem I'm having with this," Janice called out. "If someone hit Sam from behind in the location where he fell, he would have seen him standing there. Even if it was dark."

"That's true." I nodded.

"Are you sure there wasn't something else in the alley?" she asked. "A dumpster out of place, a pile of crates waiting for pick up. Anything?"

I closed my eyes and tried to remember what I'd seen. The dumpster had been against the wall where it always was and I hadn't noticed a pile of anything. I told the women as much.

"It was later than this that night," Elva pointed out. "It's just five now, and based on the information Lani has been able to gather, Sam was killed between five-thirty and six o'clock. Maybe we should wait another half hour to see if anything presents itself."

Everyone was willing to wait the additional thirty minutes. While we did they looked around. I didn't expect they'd find anything. It had been four days and any evidence that might have been there would most likely be gone. And Jason and his men had gone over everything with a fine-toothed comb. If there'd been anything to find they would have it already.

I had to hand it to the women, however. They were being thorough. Not only did they climb up onto the loading dock to get a bird's-eye view but they were bending down and looking under the dumpsters as well. I just hoped no one would break a hip or have a heart attack.

"I may not have found the murder weapon but I found half a name tag." Beth held up a small piece of blue and white that must have at one point been pinned to an employee's shirt.

"It looks like it was run over by something heavy, like a truck," Janice said.

"I wonder if it belonged to the killer," Elva murmured.

"Anyone could have lost their name tag," I said.

"Maybe, but it could be a clue," Elva persisted.

"Whoever it belonged to has a name beginning with *Br*," Beth informed us.

"Too bad it didn't start with a *Q* or a *Z*," I said. "*Br* is pretty common. It could be Brian, Brandy, Brenda, Brennan, Brent...."

"If we end up with a suspect named Brian this may be the proof we need to close the deal," Beth said.

"Okay, it's five forty-five; let's try this again," Elva suggested.

Everyone took their places and ran through the scenario we'd decided was the most likely. The overhead lights and additional darkness did lend a new feeling to the scene. If someone was wearing dark clothing, had stayed out of the path of the light, and had avoided moving around to attract attention, it was possible, although not probable, that they could have been standing out in the open but not been noticed.

"Maybe the person who hit Sam wasn't waiting in the alley," Emmy Jean announced.

"Where else could he have been?" I asked.

"Maybe someone was walking with Sam toward the building from the locker room. As they approached the loading bay door Sam saw something and turned his back on that person. Then he started to walk to whatever or whoever he'd seen, and the other person, who was now behind him, picked up the heavy object and hit him over the head."

"I suppose it could have happened that way," I said, "but if someone was walking with Sam it would most likely mean he knew the person who killed him."

No one responded. I don't think anyone wanted to consider the possibility that Sam was murdered by someone he considered a friend. Of course, the person could have been an employee who told Sam he was there to escort him to the party. If that were true the entire thing could have been a setup. I much preferred the other scenario, in which Sam stumbled onto something he shouldn't have.

"I think both scenarios have merit," Janice decided. "Maybe Sam was walking with the person who killed him or maybe he stumbled onto something and a person lurking in the shadows killed him. We just need to figure out who the two people are."

"I'll call my brother Jason. Maybe he can help make sense of this."

After a bit of discussion we decided we'd done what we could for the day. The seniors were going out for dinner, but I was tired and declined their invitation to join them. Luke was busy with his Santa deliveries, so I headed over to the locker room to shower and change into my street clothes.

"Rough day?" Makena asked. She must have just gotten off as well because she still had on her swimsuit.

"It really was."

"The beach is packed with vacationers who seem to have left their common sense at home. Cam told me there were ten rescues today between the two beaches. Most were minor, but Tommy wasn't the only one requiring CPR. Have you heard how he's doing?"

"Mitch said he's going to be fine," I said, referring to Mitch Hamilton, the lead WSO and our boss. "They're keeping him in the hospital overnight for observation. I heard you had two surfers run into each other."

"They knocked themselves out, but Shredder and some of the other surfers helped me pull them out."

Shredder was one of the other people who lived in the same condominium complex Cam, Kekoa, and I did.

"By the way, Shredder mentioned you were having a Christmas Eve party. I hoped you wouldn't mind if I came," Makena added.

I hesitated. Makena was a nice enough person, but she was Cam's girlfriend. I wondered why he hadn't invited her himself.

Makena must have noticed my hesitation because she answered my question before I could ask it. "Cam and I split up. It's all very cordial, but he's looking for something a lot more serious than I am. If you let me come to the party I promise to come alone and not antagonize Cam."

I still hesitated.

"Please. I don't have anywhere else to go."

"Okay," I agreed. I hated to think of anyone alone on Christmas Eve. "I'm sure it will be fine with Cam." Even as I said the words I hoped they were true.

"He'll be fine with it. I promise," Makena said. "If you ask me, while his ego might be bruised, he has his sights on someone else."

"Really? Who?"

Makena winked at me. "I'll never tell."

I left Makena and went into the hotel to track down Kekoa. I was feeling a bit refreshed after my shower, so I asked her if she wanted to grab dinner.

"I'd love to, but I think we should invite Cam along. He was in earlier and looked like someone had just taken away his favorite toy."

"Makena told me they split."

"That explains it. I need to run up to the business office to drop off these time cards; why don't you call Cam to see if he wants to join us? I saw him heading over to the beach bar, but I know he has his cell with him."

I called Cam while Kekoa ran her errand. He did sound a little down, but his voice seemed to pick up significantly when I mentioned dinner. He said the bar was packed, so he and I settled on buying a six pack of beer and some takeout and heading to the beach. I wanted to bring Sandy, so Cam offered to go on ahead and get a fire started. I called Luke to let him know what I was doing. If we were still at the beach when he was done with his deliveries he could join us there. If not, he could meet me at my place later.

By the time Kekoa and I picked up Sandy and headed to the beach Cam was already settled in with a large fire for warmth and a frosty beer to wash down the deli sandwiches we'd brought. I could see there was someone sitting next to him on the sand, but it wasn't until Kekoa and I got closer that I saw it was our neighbor from unit six, the man I knew only as Shredder. Sandy ran to greet Shredder's dog, Riptide, who was chasing the waves down by the waterline.

Shredder was a mysterious guy. He was nice enough, but it was obvious he was carefully guarding a secret. He fit right in with the condo family, but he never shared any personal information, and the door connecting his present to his past seemed firmly closed, with a big *stay out* sign on it.

There was a time Shredder's fierce secrecy had really bothered me, but after he saved my life on the ocean last summer, I decided he was entitled to keep his past to himself and I'd accept him as he was without worrying about who he once was or what he might have done then.

"Hey, Shredder," I greeted him. I bent down and gave him a hug. "I haven't seen you much lately."

"I've been right here like I always am. It's you who hasn't been around."

He was probably right. I spent most of my days off with Luke, and with all the extra shifts I've had on the days I did work, I hadn't been at the condo much at all.

"Cam was just catching me up on your newest murder investigation. A dead Santa in an alley is a classic."

"Unfortunately, the dead Santa happened to be a friend. He was a great guy who didn't deserve to die that way."

"Any leads?" he asked.

"Not so far." I spread out a blanket and set the sandwiches and chips I'd bought out so that everyone could help themselves. I'd had the sandwiches cut into small pieces so there was plenty to go around. "I have several theories, but so far nothing has panned out."

"You'll figure it out," Shredder assured me. "You seem to have a knack for detective work."

I certainly hoped he was right.

Chapter 9

Thursday, December 22

When the senior sleuth mystery brigade showed up at Luke's house before I had even rolled out of bed that morning, I realized if Luke and I were to have any alone time over the holidays, we needed to get this mystery wrapped up fast. He'd been up for quite a while when the women arrived because he needed to tend to the horses first thing in the morning, so he kept them entertained while I grabbed a hot cup of coffee and a quick shower.

While I appreciated the help the seniors wanted to provide, I wasn't certain there was much more we could do. The partial name tag we'd found in the alley could have been lost by an employee at any time and its mere existence didn't mean anything. Most if not all the resort employees knew about the back door and while it was frowned upon, I knew there were some who kept the door open to use the alley for smoke breaks. Still, it wouldn't hurt to check with personnel to see if anyone with a name beginning with *Br* had asked for a replacement tag that week.

Luke came into the bedroom while I was drying my hair in the adjoining bath.

"I'm sorry your house was invaded so early this morning."

"It's ten-thirty," Luke said.

I glanced at the clock. It was later than I'd thought. "I must have been really tired. Long day yesterday. But I'm surprised the gals showed up unannounced. I'm pretty sure we've followed all the leads currently available to us, so I'm not sure what they planned to accomplish today."

"I'm not sure they're here with the idea of accomplishing anything. I think they enjoy being part of a team and having something to do that has some importance."

I wrapped the cord around my dryer and put it in one of the drawers Luke had cleared out for my use. "I can understand that. I'd sort of hoped, though, that maybe you and I could spend the day together. Just us. I have a few errands to run and some last-minute Christmas shopping, so it's not like I had grand plans, but I feel like the season is passing us by and we haven't had a chance to enjoy it."

Luke came over and wrapped me in his arms, then kissed my neck. "How about we hear what they have to say and maybe even offer them an early lunch, then make it clear we have plans this afternoon that can't be put off?"

"Okay." Luke really was the sweetest man. "That sounds like a good idea. Oh," I remembered, "did you have a chance to talk to the guy all the food trucks are complaining about?"

"I did, and I can see why the other vendors are concerned. There was a line thirty people deep when I got to his truck. The guy is bright and intelligent. He uses the *burger for a buck* slogan to get people to stop by, but once he gets them there he upsells them to the eight-dollar plate that not only features twice the meat of the minuscule burger he sells for a dollar but also potato mac salad and a drink. Almost everyone took the upgrade while I was there."

I pulled my hair back and clipped a large barrette around it. "So I take it he isn't willing to fold up shop and move on."

"No, he isn't. He has a good thing going and he knows it. I don't claim to be familiar with the permit process on Oahu, but to my untrained eye he has all the permits he needs. The fact that he's using flashy signs and loss-leader marketing to pull customers away from the established food vendors isn't a reason to run the guy out of the area."

"That may be true, but the guys who work the beach have been there for a long time. They take a low-key approach to marketing. Actually, *low key* is probably a generous term. As far as I can tell, it's more like *no key*. Making the food available and people will buy it has served them well for a lot of years. It will be sad if all the vendors hop on the slash-your-neighbor's-throat bandwagon."

"I agree. Well, I'd better head down to see what the gals are up to. Meet us there when you're ready."

I straightened up the bathroom, then headed downstairs, where Luke and the seniors were discussing lunch options. They barely nodded in my direction when I appeared, but I couldn't blame them. Luke was playing the attentive and charming Southern host and the women were eating up every minute of the attention he was granting them.

"There's the sleepyhead," Tammy Rhea greeted me at last. "We thought you were going to sleep the whole day away."

"No, just half of it."

"Luke has kindly offered to make us lunch," Emmy Jean informed me. "I hope you can join us."

"I'd love to. There's still a little time before Luke and I need to head into town."

"Luke told us that you had errands to do to get ready for the party on Saturday." Elva beamed. "I want to thank you both again for doing this. We're all very grateful."

"Christmas is a time for family, no matter how you define the term."

So far so good. Luke and I had made it clear we needed to leave soon and everyone seemed content with the way things were going.

"The reason we're here is to discuss a new theory the girls and I have been discussing," Janice began.

"A new theory?"

"We were thinking about the fact that there was likely more than one person in the alley in addition to Sam when he was killed. And that it seemed Sam veered off the path he was on to approach what we hypothesized was another person or persons. Because the blow to his head came from behind we assumed there was a second person there. But what if there was just one person? What if that person said something to cause Sam to turn away and that was when he hit him?"

"I suppose that's possible, but based on the way Sam fell it seems he was looking straight ahead, not behind."

"Oh, I guess you're right. Well, it was worth mentioning."

I had to hand it to the seniors; they were a sly group. If presenting this new theory was really the main item on their agenda, they could have called one of us about it. While the theory wasn't completely far-fetched, it seemed unlikely and certainly didn't require the presence of the entire sleuthing gang.

"By the way," I said, glancing at Janice, "did you manage to find out what Ray Clark's argument with Sam was all about?"

Janice actually blushed when she looked up at me. "I did ask him about his quarrel with Sam, but all he would tell me was that he found out something about Sam that he didn't want anyone to know, and when he confronted him about it Sam became defensive. Then they argued."

"That's pretty vague," Emmy Jean pointed out. "Why didn't you push for more?"

Janice looked down at her lap. "Somehow the subject got changed and I never got the chance to pin him down. I'm having dinner with him tonight, though, so I'll see if I can get more information."

"You're having dinner with him?" Tammy Rhea asked.

"Yes, I'm having dinner with him. It's not a big deal. Ray and I are old friends."

Tammy Rhea snickered in such a way that left no doubt she knew what Janice and Ray would really be doing tonight.

We fed the seniors and sent them on their way, then Luke and I took a minute to gather our thoughts and come up with a plan for the afternoon. He wanted to stop by to speak to Komo about the food truck situation in person, which seemed like a good idea to me, and I needed to finish my Christmas shopping, which would require a trip to Honolulu, where the shopping was plentiful. Luke and I were signed up to deliver more Santa baskets that evening, so we were in something of a time crunch. Luke suggested he'd wait to speak to Komo until the following day, which would save us quite a bit of time that afternoon. I felt like we should be doing something to work on the murder case—it didn't feel right to go off shopping when nothing had been resolved—so I called Kekoa to ask her if she could find out if any resort employee with a name that began with *Br* had requested a new name tag within the past week.

"Are you ready?" Luke asked.

"Yes. I know this will be a quick trip out of necessity, but I'm looking forward to spending a few hours fighting the crowds the way normal people do this time of the year."

"You don't consider your life to be normal?"

"Not lately."

While I'd hoped to have a relaxing day free of thoughts of murder, our conversation seemed to automatically turn back to Sam's untimely death when Kekoa called me back to inform me that no one had requested a replacement name tag during the past two weeks.

"The name tag was a long shot," I admitted as we drove south toward the more populated end of the island. "The truth is, if I lost my name tag while committing a murder, I wouldn't have scooted over to personnel to ask for a new one. Too obvious."

"Is every employee required to wear a name tag?"

"Yes, in theory at least. It's not unheard of for someone to forget theirs every now and then."

"But if someone didn't have their tag for a week or more, someone would most likely say something?"

"Yeah. I guess. It depends on where the person works. If you work in one of the restaurants or at one of the customer service desks, then, yeah, their supervisor would be all over them if they didn't have a name tag. But there are some employees who never wear them. I work the beach, and given the fact I wear a bathing suit most of the time, I don't wear a name tag, although I do have one. I've also noticed the guys who work in maintenance and don't come in contact with customers don't always wear theirs, though theoretically they're supposed to."

"I wonder if it would be worth our while to get a list of all the resort employees whose name begins with *Br*," Luke mused. "Like you said, it may be a long shot, but at this point we don't have many leads."

"I guess it couldn't hurt. I'll text Kekoa to ask her to populate a list with those parameters and send it to my email."

"White Christmas" came on the car radio as I sent my request. I'd been thinking a lot about a snowy holiday ever since Luke had brought it up. "Do you have any last-minute holiday gifts to buy?" I asked.

"No. I bought gifts for my family, wrapped them, and put them under the tree before I left Texas and I took care of gifts for the people on the island before I went home. I might look for something small for the senior sleuths, although I hesitate to buy them anything in case they felt obligated to return the gesture."

"Maybe we can give them fun sleuthing gifts together as more of a thank-you for helping out. Something like a spyglass or a notebook to jot down the clues they come across."

"Are we sure we want to do something that might cause them to look as murder investigation as an ongoing activity?"

I sighed. "You might have a point. I'm always concerned that someone's going to get hurt, though it does seem they've been of help. The role-playing thing was a good idea. I'm not sure it helped us hone in on a suspect, but I do have a clearer picture in my mind of how things went down."

Luke and I sat in silence as carols continued to play. It was another beautiful day, but I could see clouds on the horizon and the weather app on my phone indicated we were in for a storm that was predicted to roll in during the overnight hours. I just hoped if it did storm hard enough to close the beaches I'd be granted an extra day off rather than being assigned to some other resort duty. So far I had Saturday, Sunday, and Monday off. Coupled with today, if I managed to get out of working tomorrow, that would give me a glorious five-day weekend. I couldn't think of anything I'd rather have for Christmas than extra time to spend with Luke, curled up in front of the tree he'd finished decorating while I'd been at work yesterday.

"Where do you want to start?" Luke asked.

I directed him to a parking garage near a shopping complex where I thought I should be able to find most of the items on my list. I usually got all my brothers the same thing. There were five of them and individual gifts were time-consuming to come up with, so somewhere along the line I came up with the idea of theme gifts. This year it was T-shirts I'd seen in an online catalog I thought they'd all get a kick out of. I'd already purchased my dad a fishing pole and my mom a set of linens I knew she'd had her eye on. I'd collected silly neighbor gifts for the tenants of the condo complex throughout the year, so I had them covered. That just left my niece and nephew, Kekoa, Cam, and Luke.

"My nephew wants a video game and my niece a baby buggy. We can get both of those at the toy store. Cam needs a new ice chest; his old one fell off the boat the last time he went fishing and ended up in the bottom of the ocean. I'm not a hundred percent sure about Kekoa, but there was this blouse she admired the last time we were shopping together. Let's start at the toy store and work our way east. Hopefully we'll get everything done before we need to head back for our volunteer duty."

I figured I'd keep my eye out for something Luke admired and then send him on an errand while I purchased it. It was a tricky Christmas for us. On one hand, it was our first together and we'd only been a couple for a short time, so I didn't want to get anything that would send a message of a commitment greater than that which we had; on the other, a can opener or a T-shirt didn't seem quite right either.

I hoped I would think of something personal but not too intimate. Maybe something to do with horses or surfing.

"By the way, I meant to tell you that I ran into Riva Spencer at the church last night," Luke informed me. "She was one of the people who volunteered to help deliver the Santa baskets."

"Geez, I totally forgot to call her back. She left a message for me two days ago, but things have been so hectic I forgot all about it. Did she have anything useful to share?"

"We only chatted for a couple of minutes, but she verified that she and Sam occasionally shared a meal, and he gave her advice about the relationships she was involved in and she helped him out with advice in turn."

"Seems like Sam had a lot of lady friends. Did she tell you anything juicy?"

"Sort of. Riva mentioned two women he'd been dueling with. One was his ex-wife and the other he'd left unnamed, although he told her the unnamed woman was becoming a pest."

"Unrequited love seems like as good a motive for murder as any."

Chapter 10

As it turned out, there were seventeen employees currently working at the Dolphin Bay Resort whose first name began with the letters *Br*. Kekoa was able to confirm that eleven of them were currently on shift and in possession of their name tags. Three were off shift, so she was unable to confirm whether they had their name tags, and another three were at work but weren't wearing their name tags. Brody Weller, who was a water safety officer like me, wore a bathing suit for most of the day, so a name tag wasn't required. Bruce Powell was a fairly new employee who worked in the maintenance department and Brenda Palmeroy was a floater who worked as a maid and a dishwasher in the main kitchen.

"Do you think this information is relevant?" Luke asked as we strolled hand in hand down the busy walkway between stores.

"I'm not sure. While it's possible *Br* lost his or her name tag in the alley on the night Sam was killed, it's just as likely the broken name tag had nothing to do with the murder. Jason did say there was no sign of a struggle." I frowned. "I guess I could ask Jason if he's identified the murder weapon. I can't believe I haven't thought to ask that before now."

"It's been a pretty hectic week."

"I'm not sure Jason will even tell me what sort of weapon was used, but it couldn't hurt to ask."

"Chances are he has a feel for the height of the person who hit Sam as well. It could help to narrow down suspects if we're ever able to hone in on anyone."

"I think honing is the problem. It would be easier if I knew for certain whether Sam was targeted or if he was in the wrong place at the wrong time."

"Maybe we should take a step back," Luke suggested. "At least for the next few days. The seniors seem to be occupied with plans for the Christmas Eve party and Jason and his team don't seem to need help from us. You look exhausted and it would be nice to simply embrace the holiday. I mean, if a clue falls into our laps, sure, we can follow it up, but right now it feels like we're spinning our wheels, chasing after leads that seem to go nowhere."

I rested my head on Luke's arm as we walked. "You're right. There's nothing we can do now anyway, so I agree we should try to find a way to relax and enjoy the holiday. I'm looking forward to delivering the Santa baskets tonight."

"I found it be very rewarding," Luke confirmed. "The church my family attends does something similar and my parents always participated when we were kids. I think my sisters still help out."

"Are you feeling sad that you aren't home this year?"

"Yes and no. There are things about Christmas in Texas I miss, but I wouldn't trade spending Christmas with you for anything. Maybe we can get some dinner after we finish the deliveries."

"I'd like that. I was thinking that… hang on." I checked my phone, which had started to vibrate, indicating I had a call. "It's Jason. I should take this."

"Let's sit over here where it's a bit less crowded."

Luke led me to an out-of-the-way bench as I answered the call. Jason asked if I'd heard from Susan Oberman, which I hadn't. Then he told me her daughter had filed a missing person's report on her.

"What?"

"Susan's daughter says she hasn't spoken to her mother since Saturday. She said they argued when they last spoke and she hasn't seen or spoken to her since."

"They have a complicated, sort of messed-up relationship. Maybe Susan is just ignoring her. This wouldn't be the first time Susan has gone off the grid for a period of time. Remember last summer when we were investigating Stuart Bronson's murder? We weren't able to get hold of her then either."

"I did think of that, which is why I haven't been overly concerned about Susan not returning my calls, but I sent a squad car over to her house. She isn't home and there are several days' worth of newspapers on the front porch."

"Did you try calling her other children? She has four children in all and the older three tend to be a lot more stable than the youngest."

"I had someone call the older three and they all reported they hadn't heard from her. However, they also said the fact that they hadn't spoken wasn't odd because they hadn't been speaking since the divorce. They all seem to blame Susan for it. At this point I'm working with the idea that Susan argued with her daughter and just needed some time away, but it might not hurt to ask the other seniors if she's been in touch."

"Yeah, I will. Is there anything else?"

"Maybe. Did you ever get around to interviewing Sam's ex, Beatrice?"

"No, not yet. She's on my list, but I didn't see her as a very high priority. I don't think of her as the killer. For one thing, she doesn't seem to have a motive."

"I thought that as well, but I have new information that's shed a different light on things. It seems Beatrice is the sole beneficiary of a life insurance policy Sam took out almost forty years ago. The current value of the policy is almost a million dollars."

"A million dollars?" I squeaked, much too loudly considering we were in a public place. "Why would she still be his beneficiary? They've been divorced a long time."

"It appears Sam took out the policy when they were newly married. He was young then, so the premiums were minimal. It's the sort of policy that increases in value as time goes by. When he and Beatrice divorced she made his continuing to make the premium payments part of the settlement. Sam had been paying on it the entire time."

"This changes things, right? I mean, before we thought Beatrice didn't have a motive to kill Sam, but a million dollars sounds like one to me."

"Yeah, me too," Jason agreed. "Except the forensic team determined that Sam's killer was at least five feet six inches tall. Beatrice Riverton is only five feet three."

"The role-playing I did with the seniors pretty much determined there was more than one person present when Sam was killed. Maybe Beatrice had an accomplice."

"Say that's true; who would help her?" Jason asked.

"I don't know. Maybe it was someone who also had something to gain, or maybe it was someone who got involved in the murder for a financial payout. The first thing we need to do is prove Beatrice was at the resort."

"*We* don't need to do anything," Jason corrected me. "The team and I will work on placing Beatrice at the resort during at the time Sam died. I found out the resort has one camera covering the front entrance. I'll have someone take a look at the video feed for that night to see if we can spot Beatrice coming or going."

"Okay. I'll be busy tonight anyway. If you make an arrest let me know. I know the seniors are anxious to have this wrapped up."

The Santa deliveries took longer than we expected, and while I had a wonderful time, I was tired and hungry by the time we had finished. Luke suggested we grab a bite at our favorite diner because neither of us had the energy to clean up and go out for a fancier meal.

"I'm not usually a fan of mashed potatoes and meat loaf, but this has to be one of the best meals I've ever had."

"Everything tastes better when you're starving," Luke pointed out.

I chewed slowly to savor every bite. It had been a long time since we'd had that early lunch with the seniors and my stomach was letting me know it had been ignored too long.

Luke glanced out of the window next to the booth where we sat. "It's starting to rain."

"We heard there was supposed to be a storm coming in. I just hope Mitch decides not to man the lifeguard towers tomorrow if the weather forecast is correct. It would be wonderful to have an extra day off rather than being reassigned."

"How do they usually handle things when the weather is too bad for you to do your shift?"

I took a bite of the potatoes I had swirled in the gravy before answering. "It depends. Sometimes he sends us home, sometimes he puts us to work in the WSO headquarters filing incident reports and that sort of thing, and sometimes the resort reassigns us to fill in if one of the other departments is short. Normally I don't mind doing whatever, but I'd love to have a nice long holiday weekend."

"You realize if the storm does blow in we might need a plan B to the pig roast the seniors came up with."

"I'm sure whatever we end up serving will be fine with everyone."

I watched the rain as it slowly increased in strength from a few sprinkles to a steady downpour. Of course, in Hawaii a downpour could be over almost as soon as it began, so it wasn't a given that I'd be called off work the next day. I was contemplating the idea of dessert when Jason texted to let me know the video feed had confirmed that Beatrice had come to the resort on Saturday. That didn't prove she'd killed Sam, but it was a step in solving what had turned out to be a complicated murder case.

Did you ask her why she was there? I texted.

She said Sam had forgotten his hat and belt when he picked up the Santa outfit at her house, Jason answered.

I supposed that was credible.

Did the camera catch her arriving and leaving? I wondered.

Just arriving. Her car went through the entrance gate at 5:20.

Okay, that fit the timeline. If Sam had begun to dress and realized he'd forgotten part of his costume he could very well have called Beatrice to asked her to bring it. Of course, when Jason had spoken to Beatrice in the first place she'd told him she'd been at home the night Sam died. If she was truly innocent why hadn't she mentioned that she'd gone to the resort? Jason texted back to add that she knew it would make her look guilty.

The question was, did she look guilty because she was, or did she look guilty because, like Sam, she'd been in the wrong place at the wrong time?

"Based on her height, Beatrice couldn't have killed Sam herself. What do you want to bet one of the four men from the senior center acted as her accomplice?" I asked Luke.

"Makes sense, but which one?"

"I'm not sure. We suspect Walt held a grudge against Sam because he believed he'd gotten between him and Tina, the woman from the soup kitchen. I'd observed myself that Gil and Sam didn't always get along. As far as I know there wasn't a woman involved in that instance but more of a natural rivalry between two very competitive men who both like to win. I don't know Ted well, but I have no reason to believe he had anything against Sam. And then there's Steven. He seemed honest when he said he didn't kill his brother, but you never know what's truly in someone's heart."

"Steven did seem to have a soft spot for Beatrice," Luke said.

"And he gained financially from Sam's death," I added.

"And Steven and Beatrice were brother- and sister-in-law for twenty years, so they must know each other well."

I frowned. "Do you think that's what happened? Do you think Steven and Beatrice teamed up to kill Sam? The more I think about it, the more sense it seems to make."

"They would have had to come up with a plan pretty quickly," Luke pointed out.

"True. But there were several hours between my call to Sam about covering for Santa and the time he arrived at the resort. The idea might have been Steven's initially. He heard about it first and, according to what he told us, declined Sam's offer to be his guest at the resort."

"Which makes sense if he wanted to be able move around freely."

"So he asks some of the other guys to come along to play a prank on Sam, thereby giving him an excuse to be there," I theorized.

"Then he calls Beatrice, who wants in on the action, and they come up with a plan after Steven finds out exactly where Sam will be and when he'll be there."

"Steven said coming to the resort was Walt's idea," I recalled.

"But we never confirmed that with Walt."

The more I thought about it, the more I liked this theory. Both Steven and Beatrice had reason to resent Sam and both gained financially by his death. Beatrice could have positioned herself at the loading dock so Sam would turn away from Steven, who I assumed had accompanied Sam as he walked toward the back door of the building where the event was being held. Once his attention was focused on Beatrice, Steven picked up something he'd probably planted there earlier and hit Sam over the head with it. Sam fell, Beatrice left the resort, and Steven returned to his friends, claiming he had stepped out for a smoke.

"I need to call Jason."

Chapter 11

Friday, December 23

As it turned out, Jason liked my theory, but he said he still needed to prove it; coming up with a scenario that made sense wasn't enough for an arrest. He'd work on it and I promised to stay out of it and let him do his job. Given the state of my fatigue and the upcoming holiday, I was happy to do just that. Having figured things out gave me a sense of satisfaction, even if he would be the one involved in the actual takedown.

"I don't see why Mitch is making us come in," I complained to Sandy about the fact that, although it was raining cats and dogs, my boss was still requiring all the WSOs to show up for work as scheduled. "Sometimes I think he just likes to torture us."

Sandy tilted his head, which indicated he was listening, although I was certain he had no idea what I was rambling on about.

"It would be such a perfect day to sleep in. Nothing to do, nowhere to go, but no, Mitch has to ruin what could have been a perfectly wonderful day off."

"Are you almost ready in there?" Cam called through the closed door of my bedroom. We were on the same shift and were planning to drive in to work together.

"Yeah. Almost. I just need two minutes."

"We don't have two minutes. Get a move on or we'll be late."

Cam was a nice guy and truly one of my best friends next to Kekoa, but he could be pushy at times. I didn't see what difference it was going to make if we were a few minutes late. There was no way they'd be manning the towers today, which meant that if Mitch was making us come in there was most likely filing in our future. Talk about a boring way to spend an otherwise dreary day.

"Housekeeping?" I screeched. "You want me to help out in housekeeping?"

Okay, this was even worse than filing. I'd been assigned to one of the reception desks a time or two when the weather had been too bad to man the towers, but housekeeping? Why hadn't I just called in sick?

"The housekeeping staff is shorthanded, the resort is booked solid, and you have nothing else to do."

"Oh but I do," I tried to convince the man I normally referred to as boss or sometimes friend but now considered a pain in my backside. "I'm sure there must be filing that needs to be done."

"Makena is on the filing."

"Someone needs to answer the phones. Just because we aren't out on the beach doesn't mean there won't be an emergency."

"Cam's on phones."

"Scheduling?" I tried weakly.

"Done. They're expecting you on the fourth floor. Ask for Flo. She's the supervisor for this shift."

I tossed my backpack into a corner a lot harder than I needed to. Mitch gave me a stern look I was tempted to return with a middle-finger salute but somehow managed to refrain from doing anything that might very well get me fired.

"And Lani," Mitch added after I turned to leave, "try to have a good attitude. The women you'll be working with do that job every day. If you make it seem like eight hours in hell you'll offend them."

I suppose he had a point. It certainly wasn't Flo's fault or her crew's that I'd been assigned a simply horrible job on an equally horrible day.

As I got off the elevator on four it occurred to me that the housekeeping office wasn't the only one on this floor; the security office was located there as well. Although I felt confident Jason and I had identified Sam's killer, we'd never answered the question of the missing video feed or the shadow on the loading dock right before Sam's death. I didn't know it for certain, but I was confident neither Steven nor Beatrice were capable of editing secure video content from a remote location, nor were they likely to have been inside the main building prior to Sam's death. I hoped my buddy Bill was on duty. If he was maybe I could convince him to engage in a little cybersleuthing.

"Don't tell me there's been another murder," Bill said as I walked in.

"No, not another one. It turns out I still have some questions about the other one. I had a little time on my hands and thought that maybe..." I let the thought trail off.

"You thought I'd be interested in risking my job so you can assuage your curiosity."

"Exactly." I smiled and pulled up a chair next to his.

Bill groaned, but he didn't throw me out, which was something.

"What are we looking for now?"

"A couple of things. First of all, you said there are cameras in the restaurants. Does that include the pool bar?"

"Yeah, there's one in the bar."

"Can you pull up the footage from December 17 at around five p.m.?"

Bill typed a set of commands into his keyboard. "Here you go. The pool bar at five p.m. on December 17."

Luckily, the camera was pointing toward the table where Steven and his friends were sitting. I watched as they laughed and pounded down drinks. The video didn't include audio, so I had to guess what they might be saying.

"Can you fast forward slowly so that we can see what's happening but at an accelerated speed?"

"Sure. Anything for the pretty girl who's going to be responsible for my impending unemployment."

"Don't be so dramatic. You aren't going to get fired. Stop right there." The video stopped. "What time is that?"

"Five-seventeen."

Steven had gotten up and left the group at five-nineteen. A little early but still feasible. "Continue forward until this man returns to the group." I pointed at Steven.

"Five twenty-eight."

Dang. That was quicker than I'd expected. It would have been difficult to walk Santa over to the loading dock, kill him, and return to the bar in less than ten minutes. Nine minutes to smoke a cigarette—which is what he'd told me he'd done when he left the others—was just about right.

After Steven returned Walt and Gil both got up and left as well. Walt was back in six minutes and Gil in twelve. Ted didn't get up to call his wife until well out of the window of time we'd determined Sam had died.

"Is there a way to track someone's movements through the resort?"

"I guess. If the person moves into locations where there are cameras."

"See this man?" I pointed at Steven again. "Can you tell where he went when he left the bar?"

Bill focused in on Steven and then pulled up the camera just outside the building for the same time. We could see Steven exit the building, pull a pack of cigarettes out of his pocket, and then head toward the beach, away from the scene of the crime. He returned nine minutes later from the direction in which he'd walked. It was beginning to look as if Steven hadn't killed Sam after all.

Dang, and it had been such a good theory.

"Can you see if you can follow this man when he leaves?" I pointed at Gil. Twelve minutes was still a pretty tight window of time to follow Sam to the loading dock, hit him with a heavy object, and make it back to the bar, though not impossible. As far as I knew, Gil didn't have a problem with Sam, but, as I had learned over the past few days, there was a lot more going on with Sam than I'd ever imagined.

"Can you pick him up after he turns onto the walkway?"

After Gil left the bar he turned in the right direction to be going to the alley behind the loading dock, but he'd taken a walkway rather than continuing down the main thoroughfare connecting the two areas, so it wasn't possible to follow him.

"If he comes back onto the main thoroughfare after he passes the locker room I might be able to pick him up."

We watched and waited, but we never saw him arrive at the intersection where the walkway and the driveway adjoined.

"I can scan the feed to see if I pick up any of these men in a different part of the resort if you'd like."

"I would like. Thanks. Call my cell if you find anything."

As much as I hated to do it, I realized if I wanted to still be employed at the resort after the holidays I'd best check in with Flo and learn my fate.

"You're late," Flo greeted me.

"I had to stop off at the bathroom," I lied.

Flo eyed me up and down but didn't respond in any other way.

"I'm here now, though," I said in an attempt to lighten the mood. "Ready and willing to work."

"Fine. Here's a list of chores that need to be attended to. Mostly deliveries. And here's a master key to all the rooms."

That didn't sound too bad. Making deliveries would be much better than scrubbing and cleaning. I looked at the list. Several rooms needed extra towels, another a hideaway bed, and several others snacks for the honor bar. Piece of cake. I confirmed with Flo where I could find all the supplies I'd need and then set out to do my job.

Somewhere around the fifth room I entered I realized how very easy it would be for someone who was doing this sort of thing to be the thief who'd been making off with guests' jewelry for the past several weeks. The maids worked in teams, which would make a theft harder to pull off, but someone who was simply making deliveries could slip in and out unnoticed. And the perfect thing about this theory was that someone with a master key could slip into any room they wanted, not only those they'd been assigned to enter.

I wondered if Jason had considered this. Probably. Still, it couldn't hurt to give him a call to run it past him. I dialed the number for his cell and waited for him to pick up. I got his voice mail.

"Hey, big brother. I've got some news and a theory to run past you. I'm at work right now, but—" I stopped talking abruptly. I could hear someone on the other side of the door leading out to the hallway. I was about to go over to open it when an inner voice told me to hide instead.

I hid behind the floor-to-ceiling drapes and watched as the new maintenance man, Bruce Powell, came into the room. I was about to make my presence known when he pulled out a phone and began talking.

"Okay, I'm in the room. What am I looking for?"

I watched as he listened to the reply before walking over to the closet and opening the door.

"Yeah, I see it," he said. "I'll meet you in ten."

I couldn't resist a peek as Bruce did something inside the closet. It occurred to me that the safe was in the closet and perhaps he was the thief Jason had been after, but he was a maintenance man; he might just be fixing a loose closet rod.

When he stepped out of the closet with a tennis bracelet with so many diamonds it had to be worth tens of thousands of dollars I knew I had my answer.

I watched and waited until Bruce left the room. Jason wouldn't like it, but I knew I had to follow him. I was still on the line with Jason's voice mail, so I quickly filled him in on what I was doing and then hurried to the door. I looked up and down the hall but couldn't determine where he'd gone. The elevator stopped on the garage floor, so I guessed he'd gone to his car. I entered the hall, hurried toward the elevator, and pushed the button for the garage, where I hoped I'd be able to find him.

The problem was, he found me. The moment the elevator doors opened he grabbed me and forced me into the back of a van he had waiting just outside the elevator.

"How did you know I was following you?" I demanded after he took off toward the exit of the multilevel garage.

"The tips of your tennis shoes were peeking out when you were standing behind the drape, so I knew you were watching me."

Drat! I should have realized. "I saw you take that bracelet."

"Figured."

I looked around the van. There was only the one door and it didn't open from the inside. I looked at the old blankets I was sitting on. They not only stank to high heaven but appeared to be covered in blood.

This couldn't get any worse.

I reached for my phone but realized I must have dropped it along the way. "My brother is a cop and you're going to be in a lot of trouble when he catches up with you."

"He won't catch up with me because he won't know you saw me take the bracelet or that I have you. All he'll know for certain is that his little sister died in a terrible accident."

Hmm. That didn't sound good. "So I take it you're planning to kill me."

"I'm afraid I have no other choice. It's a shame. I've been watching you snooping around ever since the old man died. Despite the way this has to end I want you to know I admire your spunk."

"What if I hadn't followed you to the garage?"

"I knew you would. Remember, I've been watching you. I know you're the nosy type who won't let anything go. Besides, you aren't normal. Another trait I happen to admire."

"I am so normal." Out of everything he had said, this was what stuck in my craw most. Not normal my ass.

"Normal? Really? I just tossed you into a van. You have no means of escape and no idea what I'm going to do with you once we get where we're going. Most normal women would be hollering and crying, but here you are, interrogating me like you're the one holding the gun."

I guess he had a point. Maybe I wasn't normal.

"You know, I think we may have gotten off on the wrong foot," I tried. "I'm a reasonable person. I guess I get the whole steal-from-the-rich point of view. I mean, seriously, how many diamonds does a person need? Am I right? How about we forget about this whole thing? You let me go and I won't tell my brother or anyone else what I saw in that room."

He just laughed.

"You know, you're making a mistake," I tried again. "So far all you've done is steal some jewelry. Even if I did tell the cops what I know you're looking at a few years behind bars. But if you kill someone— mainly me—well, that's a different story entirely."

He didn't answer.

"Trust me: You really don't want to cross the line between being a thief and being a murderer."

"Too late. It's a line I already crossed, so save your breath." He chuckled as he made a sharp turn that sent me flying across the van.

I put my hands out in front of me, trying to stop myself from smashing into the metal paneling.

"Already crossed?" I grabbed my shoulder as a sharp pain radiated down to my elbow. "What are you talking about?"

"I thought you'd figured it out. Maybe you aren't as smart as I thought you were."

Figured it out? Of course: the shadow on the video feed the night Sam was killed. Bruce must have been the one who went into the alley. He'd probably met with a partner or maybe a buyer for his ill-gotten gains. Sam had wandered into the alley on his way to the back door and was killed to silence him.

"You killed Santa!"

"I didn't kill him. Would have, but the dame he was with got to him first."

"You must mean Beatrice."

"Didn't catch her name before I stuck a knife in her neck. She had spunk too. In fact, she put up quite a fight. Now shut up. This conversation is getting on my nerves."

If Bruce had killed the person who'd killed Sam it couldn't have been Beatrice; she was still alive. The questions now were who was missing and what had happened to her body?

"Susan. You killed Susan."

"Like I said, I didn't catch her name."

"I don't get it. Why did you kill the woman who was with Sam? And what did you do with her body? And why move her body but leave Sam lying in the alley?"

"You sure do talk a lot for someone who should be praying right about now." Bruce pulled the van off the highway onto a dirt road. I thought we were probably nearing the end of the road and, most likely, the end of my life. I noticed the ocean in the distance. My only hope was to catch Bruce off guard and make a run for the water. If I could make it there I could survive. The water was, after all, my element.

Luckily for me, Bruce chose to park the van near an old shack that was perched on the water's edge. That would work in my favor. He opened the side door and demanded I get out. The overconfident idiot didn't even have a gun. He probably figured he wouldn't need one against a little girl like me. Once I was on the ground he grabbed my arm. I pretended I was about to puke, so he let go of my arm and took a step back to avoid the vomit. I kicked him in the groin as hard as I could, then took off running toward the water. He must have found that gun I hadn't seen before because I heard bullets hitting the water all around me as I dove deeper and deeper.

Chapter 12

December 24

I was dreaming I was drowning. I could see the surface of the water just above me, but no matter how hard I tried I couldn't pull away from the force that was pulling me under. I knew I was going to die, but somehow, in that moment, in that dream, I found acceptance in the knowledge that I had done everything I could to right a great wrong. I felt the reserve to hold my breath waver as I prepared myself to accept death. It wouldn't be so bad. I imagined in death the noise of the world simply fades away. I liked the quiet.

"Lani. Sweetheart. Wake up."

I felt myself pulled gently out of my dream. Someone was holding me. I began to struggle as I imagined myself being held under the surface of the water.

"Come on, babe. Wake up. It's me, Luke."

I struggled to open my eyes. I felt confused, but not so much so that I didn't realize I was somewhere in the dark but not under the water, where I was certain I'd been just a second ago.

"Luke?"

"You were having a bad dream. It's okay. Everything's okay. I'm here with you. You're safe."

I closed my eyes again. I could feel the damp sheets beneath my body, which was covered in sweat. I knew I was in Luke's bed, but I wondered how I'd gotten there. The last thing I remembered was being pulled down into the depths of the ocean.

I could feel the tears on my cheeks as Luke pulled me into his arms. He was whispering in my ear, in an attempt, I thought, to calm me and slow my racing heart.

"I was in the water," I murmured.

"That was yesterday. You're safe now. Do you remember?"

"There was someone shooting at me." I tried to clear the jumbled images in my mind. "Bruce. He killed Susan and tried to kill me."

"He tried, but you got away."

"Swimming. I swam away."

"Yes, you did."

"But I drowned."

"No." I could feel moisture on my cheek, which was resting on Luke's neck. I suspected this time the tears were his, not mine. "You swam for at least two miles before you found a safe place to leave the water, but you made it. You didn't drown."

It was beginning to come back to me. Bruce had followed me for a while, shooting bullets into the water, but I'd managed to outlast him. If I hadn't been in such good shape, if I hadn't swum almost every day of my life, I never would have made it.

"Jason came for me."

"Yes, he did. When he got your message and realized what had happened he dispatched every cop on the north shore to look for you. He was bent on rescuing you, but you didn't need it. You rescued yourself."

I felt myself begin to relax as Luke stroked my hair. I did remember. Bruce had been shooting at me while I tried to get away and kept on swimming. I swam far enough out into the sea to be out of range and then paralleled the beach until I was certain he'd given up. Once I found a sheltered place to get out of the water, I swam toward the beach and then walked out to the road, where Jason had found me hitchhiking. He'd insisted on taking me to the hospital to be checked out, but I was fine, so eventually he agreed to let me go to Luke's. Cam and Kekoa were here as well. Jason didn't want me to go home until he tracked Bruce down, which he'd finally accomplished sometime in the middle of the night.

"Cam and Kekoa?"

"They went to work," Luke answered. "You're safe. You're all safe. Bruce is behind bars and it's been confirmed that the man he was working with to fence the stolen jewelry is cooperating completely as part of a plea bargain."

I focused on my breathing as I let the memories of the previous day come flooding back. As it turned out, Susan had been walking with Sam that night for some reason. We weren't certain what had happened because neither of them were alive to tell us, but we suspected Susan must have sought Sam out for a private conversation during the time she'd told the others she had to take a call from her daughter. Bruce did say Sam and Susan had been arguing when they arrived in the alley, where Bruce was meeting the man who'd agreed to fence his stolen property. Sam turned away from Susan to speak to Bruce, but she tried to grab him and pull him back. Sam shook her off and continued on toward where Bruce was standing. Susan had picked up a heavy metal rod and hit Sam, screaming all the while that she was done being ignored and he was going to take responsibility for what he'd done.

Susan had kept on screaming at Sam even after he'd fallen to the ground. Bruce was afraid she'd bring unwanted attention to the alley, so he'd killed her and stuffed her body in his van. He'd left it in the shack where he'd tried to take me. Jason's men had found her body after I'd described the place where I'd managed to get away from Bruce.

All in all, yesterday had been a pretty horrible end to a pretty awful week.

"The senior brigade is downstairs to help us get ready for the party," Luke said when I'd finally stopped shaking. "I can send them away. I'm sure they'll understand if we decide to cancel the party."

"No," I said. "Don't cancel it. The senior community has suffered a huge loss this week. First Sam, then Susan. I think we could all use some holiday cheer. I'll be fine. After coffee. And a shower."

"If you're sure. You hop in the shower and I'll bring you up a cup of coffee."

I smiled at Luke and tried not to let him know my entire body hurt. Between being thrown around in the van and then swimming for who knew how many miles,

I felt like I'd been run over by a truck. But today was Christmas Eve and I wanted to step out of the darkness and remember everything wonderful life had to offer.

"I have to hand it to you; despite everything that's happened this week you managed to pull off the holiday party of the season," Kekoa said.

"Luke and the seniors have been working like maniacs all day. I can't believe how much they managed to get done in such a short period of time. It really does seem that everyone has been able to put the horror of the past week behind them and embrace the friends and family who are gathered here today."

"Did you ever figure out why Susan killed Sam?"

"We can't be certain, but Janice spoke to Susan's sister, who told her that she and Sam had had a fling that was the catalyst behind her divorce. Apparently, the whole thing had been very hard on her. Not only had her husband left her but her adult children blamed her for the breakup of the family and refused to speak to her. Then, to make matters worse, Sam dumped Susan after the damage was done. Susan's sister thinks the stress had been building and eventually she snapped."

"It's such a shame. So many lives ruined and for what?"

"I hear ya."

Kekoa hugged me. "I'm so glad Jason caught up with Bruce. I was so worried he'd come after you to try again."

"At this point all, or at least most, of the bad guys are behind bars."

"Most?"

"They still aren't certain who altered the video feed. Neither Bruce nor his partner seem skilled enough to have done it. Jason thinks it might have been Titan after all, but he can't prove it."

"Why would Titan alter the video feed?"

"For money. If he figured out it was Bruce behind the thefts he might have agreed to turn a blind eye for a payout."

"I guess that makes sense. But how will Jason prove it one way or the other?"

"I'm not sure he can. I'd like to see justice prevail, but for now I plan to relax and enjoy this fabulous party."

"Well, I'm grateful Luke suggested it. With my mom on the mainland visiting my sister and my dad who knows where, I'm very happy to have had somewhere to go."

"By the way, I meant to tell you, you're invited to my parents' tomorrow. It won't be the whole family, but Mom's doing a dinner."

"Actually," Kekoa said, "I have plans."

"Plans? With who?"

Kekoa glance across the room to the spot where Cam was chatting with Luke. I glanced back and forth between the two.

"Cam?"

"It's not a big deal. Cam didn't have anywhere to go and neither did I. We're both working the morning shift, so we decided to go out together when we get off."

"That makes sense," I said, even as it dawned on me that Kekoa was the *someone else* Makena had been referring to when she'd told me she'd broken up with Cam. "I need another drink. Do you want anything?"

"No," Kekoa answered as she continued to look at Cam. "I'm fine."

Cam and Kekoa. Who would have thought? Sure, they got along well. The three of us had been best friends since we were kids. I suppose I should have seen it coming. I thought back to our trip to Dracula's castle last October and remembered the way Cam had taken care of Kekoa. I guess it did occur to me back then that there might be more between them, but then we'd come home and returned to our lives as usual, so I figured I'd been wrong.

"Penny for your thoughts," Luke said as he bent over and gave me a gentle kiss on the lips.

"I think there might be something going on between Cam and Kekoa."

"You mean you're just figuring that out? For someone who can track down even the slyest killer you seem to be a little slow when it comes to love."

I put my arms around Luke's neck and looked him in the eye. "I might be slow to catch on, but once I do I really know how to take control."

Luke smiled. "You don't say."

"I do say. In fact, when this party is over I plan to show you exactly how in control I can be."

Luke lifted his hands to my face. He slowly pulled my head to his. Then he leaned forward and kissed me so softly I was certain I must have imagined it. I felt my heart begin to pound as I realized the promise wrapped up in that one Christmas kiss.

Recipes

French Toast—submitted by Joyce Aiken

Cranberry Mellow Salad—submitted by Janel Flynn

Marie's Gingersnaps—submitted by Marie Rice

Chocolate Cookies—submitted by Pam Curran

Candy Cane Snowballs—submitted by Kim Davis

Chocolate Cherry Cake—submitted by Connie Correll

Dutch Chocolate Cherry (or Cranberry) Cookies—submitted by Joanne Kocourek

Rum Bundt Cake—submitted by Vivian Shane

French Toast

Submitted by Joyce Aiken

This recipe came from a co-worker. It's nice because you make it the day before company comes.

12 slices bread
1 8-oz. pkg. cream cheese
8 eggs
1 cup milk
½ cup maple syrup

In buttered 9 x 13 pan, break up 6 slices of bread to cover the bottom of the pan. Cut cream cheese into chunks and place over the bread. Break up the rest of bread and place on top. Mix eggs, milk, and maple syrup in a bowl and pour over. Cover and refrigerate overnight. Bake at 375 degrees for 20–25 minutes with cover on. Remove cover and bake another 20 minutes.

Cranberry Mellow Salad

Submitted by Janel Flynn

2 cups (½ lb.) raw cranberries
4 cups (½ lb.) minimarshmallows
½ cup sugar
¼ cup chopped nuts (walnuts work best)
¼ cup chopped apple (keep skins on)
1 small can diced pineapple (fresh pineapple tastes best)
1 cup cream, whipped

Grind cranberries. Stir in marshmallows and sugar. Chill overnight so marshmallows will absorb the juice. Add nuts and apples and pineapple, fold in whipped cream. Chill thoroughly. Makes 10–12 servings

Marie's Gingersnaps

Submitted by Marie Rice

I know the *snap* part of the name is supposed to indicate a hard, crunchy cookie, but I prefer my gingersnaps to be a bit chewy. ~smile~

¾ cup shortening
1 cup brown sugar
¼ cup molasses
1 egg
2¼ cups all-purpose flour
2 tsp. baking soda
1 tsp. ground ginger
1 tsp. ground cinnamon
½ tsp. ground cloves
Granulated sugar for rolling

Preheat oven to 350 degrees.

In a large bowl, cream together the first four ingredients until fluffy. In a separate bowl, sift the remaining ingredients together. Stir the flour mixture into the molasses mixture.

Lightly spray baking sheets. Form dough into small balls and roll in granulated sugar. Place 2 inches apart on the sheets. Bake for about 10 minutes or until the desired firmness/hardness. (For crunchier cookies, leave in oven for longer.)

Cool for a couple of minutes on baking sheet and then move cookies to cooling rack to finish cooling. If reusing the baking sheet for another batch, use spatula to scrap the sheet and then respray before placing more cookie dough on the sheet.

Makes about 5 dozen cookies.

Chocolate Cookies

Submitted by Pam Curran

This recipe came from a home economics teacher at one of the school districts in which I taught and who was working with my husband when he was in administration. We still keep in touch even though we don't live in the same town. She was known for her yummy sweets.

Melt together:

1 large pkg. chocolate chips (8 oz.)
3 tbs. margarine

Add:

1 can Eagle Brand milk
2 cups chopped pecans, mixed with 1 cup flour

Mix well. Let stand 30 minutes. Roll into small balls. Bake at 300 degrees for 10–12 minutes.

Melt the chocolate chips and margarine in the microwave. Also, using a melon ball scoop to shape the cookies helps out. These are very rich.

Candy Cane Snowballs

Submitted by Kim Davis

3 cups all-purpose flour
1 tsp. baking powder
¾ tsp. sea salt
1½ cups confectioner's sugar
1¼ cups unsalted butter, at room temperature
1 egg, at room temperature
1 tsp. peppermint extract
1 tsp. vanilla extract
1 cup peppermint candy canes, finely crushed
Granulated sugar for rolling cookies

Preheat oven to 350 degrees.
In a medium-sized bowl, whisk the flour, baking powder, and sea salt together. Set aside.
In the bowl of a standing mixer, beat the powdered sugar and butter together until creamy, about 2 minutes.

Add the egg and beat until well combined.

Add the peppermint extract and vanilla and stir to thoroughly combine.
Slowly add the flour mixture and stir until well blended on low speed.

Remove the bowl from the standing mixer and add the crushed peppermint candy, stirring into the cookie dough by hand.

Form the dough into 1-inch balls and roll in granulated sugar.

Place on a parchment-lined baking sheet, 12 cookies per sheet. Bake for 10–12 minutes. The bottoms of the cookies should just start to be showing golden color.

Allow the cookies to cool on the baking sheet for 5 minutes, then remove and cool completely.
Makes approximately 5 dozen cookies, depending on size.

Tips:
If the dough is too sticky when rolling into balls, refrigerate for 1 hour.
You can substitute Andes Peppermint Crunch baking pieces for the crushed candy canes, if desired.

Chocolate Cherry Cake

Submitted by Connie Correll

Mix these ingredients together; bake at 350 degrees for about 30 minutes.

1 cup sugar
½ tsp. salt
½ cup butter (real stuff)
1 egg beaten
¾ cup sour milk
1 tsp. baking soda
1 square of melted chocolate
1 small bottle maraschino cherries (drained but keep the juice)
¼ cup cherry juice
1½ cups flour
½ cup walnuts

My grandfather loved this cake—well, he loved cherries—so Gram would make this more often than just his birthday or holidays. I had to look up how to make "sour milk," so this is what you do: for 1 cup sour milk or buttermilk use 1 cup whole milk with 1 tbs. lemon juice or vinegar, stirred together.

Dutch Chocolate Cherry (or Cranberry) Cookies

Submitted by Joanne Kocourek

These are delicious (I divide the dough and add dried cranberries to half and dried cherries to half so everyone is happy). I made dozens of them last year for gifts to co-workers and neighbors. Great rich chocolate cookies with a hint of cinnamon. The cherries and/or cranberries give them a great chewy texture, combined with a delightful hint of cinnamon, coffee, and chocolate.

2 cups flour
½ cup Dutch-processed cocoa powder (must be Dutch cocoa powder for the best flavor)
1 tsp. ground cinnamon
½ tsp. baking powder
½ tsp. baking soda
½ cup butter, softened
½ cup vegetable shortening
½ cup granulated sugar
1 cup firmly packed light brown sugar
2 large eggs
1 tsp. vanilla extract
1 tsp. instant coffee granules
1 cup white chocolate chips
1 cup semisweet chocolate chips
1 cup dried cranberries or dried cherries (or ½ cup of each)

Preheat oven to 350 F. Line baking sheets with parchment paper.

Sift together flour, cocoa powder, ground cinnamon, baking powder and baking soda, and set aside.

In a large bowl, use an electric mixer to beat butter, shortening, granulated sugar, and brown sugar until light and fluffy. Add eggs, one at a time, mixing until fully combined before next addition.

In a small cup, mix together the vanilla and the coffee until the coffee is dissolved, then add to the butter mixture; beat to combine.

Gradually add dry ingredients, mixing until combined.

Stir in by hand white chocolate chips, semisweet chocolate chips, and dried cranberries.
Drop 1 tbs. of dough at a time onto baking sheets, spacing cookies about 2 inches apart. Bake for 8–10 minutes or until firm. Let cool for 1 minute, then transfer to a wire rack to cool completely.
Store in airtight containers at room temperature for up to 1 month.
Makes approximately 48 cookies.

Rum Bundt Cake

Submitted by Vivian Shane

Cake:

1 cup chopped pecans
18½ oz.-pkg. yellow cake mix with pudding
3 eggs
½ cup cold water
⅓ cup vegetable oil
½ cup dark rum

Glaze:

1 stick butter
1 cup sugar
¼ cup water
¾ tsp. sea salt
⅓ cup dark rum

Preheat oven to 325 degrees. Grease and flour Bundt pan. Sprinkle nuts in the bottom of the pan. Mix cake ingredients together and pour over nuts. Bake for one hour. Cool and invert onto a serving plate.

For glaze, melt butter in saucepan; stir in sugar and water. Boil for 5 minutes, stirring constantly. Remove from heat and stir in sea salt and rum.

Prick the top of the cake with a fork and spoon/brush glaze evenly over top and sides. Allow the cake to absorb the glaze, then repeat until glaze is used up.

Books by Kathi Daley

Come for the murder, stay for the romance.

Zoe Donovan Cozy Mystery:

Halloween Hijinks
The Trouble With Turkeys
Christmas Crazy
Cupid's Curse
Big Bunny Bump-off
Beach Blanket Barbie
Maui Madness
Derby Divas
Haunted Hamlet
Turkeys, Tuxes, and Tabbies
Christmas Cozy
Alaskan Alliance
Matrimony Meltdown
Soul Surrender
Heavenly Honeymoon
Hopscotch Homicide
Ghostly Graveyard
Santa Sleuth
Shamrock Shenanigans
Kitten Kaboodle
Costume Catastrophe

Candy Cane Caper
Holiday Hangover – *January 2017*

Zimmerman Academy The New Normal

Ashton Falls Cozy Cookbook

Tj Jensen Paradise Lake Mysteries by Henery Press
Pumpkins in Paradise
Snowmen in Paradise
Bikinis in Paradise
Christmas in Paradise
Puppies in Paradise
Halloween in Paradise
Treasure in Paradise – *April 2017*

Whales and Tails Cozy Mystery:
Romeow and Juliet
The Mad Catter
Grimm's Furry Tail
Much Ado About Felines
Legend of Tabby Hollow
Cat of Christmas Past
A Tale of Two Tabbies
The Great Catsby
Count Catula

Seacliff High Mystery:
The Secret
The Curse
The Relic
The Conspiracy
The Grudge

Sand and Sea Hawaiian Mystery:
Murder at Dolphin Bay
Murder at Sunrise Beach
Murder at the Witching Hour
Murder at Christmas

Road to Christmas Romance:
Road to Christmas Past

Kathi Daley lives with her husband, kids, grandkids, and Bernese mountain dogs in beautiful Lake Tahoe. When she isn't writing, she likes to read (preferably at the beach or by the fire), cook (preferably something with chocolate or cheese), and garden (planting and planning, not weeding). She also enjoys spending time on the water when she's not hiking, biking, or snowshoeing the miles of desolate trails surrounding her home.

Kathi uses the mountain setting in which she lives, along with the animals (wild and domestic) that share her home, as inspiration for her cozy mysteries.

Kathi is a top 100 mystery writer for Amazon and she won the 2014 award for both Best Cozy Mystery Author and Best Cozy Mystery Series.

She currently writes five series: Zoe Donovan Cozy Mysteries, Whales and Tails Island Mysteries, Sand and Sea Hawaiian Mysteries, Tj Jensen Paradise Lake Mysteries, and Seacliff High Teen Mysteries.

Giveaway:

I do a giveaway for books, swag, and gift cards every week in my newsletter, *The Daley Weekly*
http://eepurl.com/NRPDf

Other links to check out:
Kathi Daley Blog – publishes each Friday
http://kathidaleyblog.com
Webpage – www.kathidaley.com
Facebook at Kathi Daley Books –
www.facebook.com/kathidaleybooks
Kathi Daley Teen –
www.facebook.com/kathidaleyteen
Kathi Daley Books Group Page –
https://www.facebook.com/groups/569578823146850/
E-mail – kathidaley@kathidaley.com
Goodreads –
https://www.goodreads.com/author/show/7278377.Kathi_Daley
Twitter at Kathi Daley@kathidaley –
https://twitter.com/kathidaley
Amazon Author Page –
https://www.amazon.com/author/kathidaley

BookBub –
https://www.bookbub.com/authors/
kathi-daley
Pinterest –
http://www.pinterest.com/kathidale
y/

Made in the USA
Middletown, DE
17 September 2018